CAPTURING AVA

SHADOWS OF DESIRE

BOOK *1*

CALIA QUINN

copyrights

CONTENT WARNING:

Capturing Ava is intended for 18+ due to the strong adult themes.

Due to the sensitive content in this book, a list of content warnings are posted below.

WARNING:

Breath play; kidnapping; drug use; violence; torture; strong sexual themes; trauma; close proximity; close impact play; psychological trauma; stalking; dub-con;

non-con;

While there are a fair few CW listed for Capturing Ava, the love that grows between the main characters makes me swoon!

Capturing Ava does end on a cliff hanger.

I hope you fall for Chase as much as I did!

Calia Quinn XOXO

Run,
Little Beast,
Run

Beast
Little

You can run,
But you can't hide

preface

Capturing Ava is a work of fiction and follows Ava and Chase, the two main characters.

When I started writing this piece, I put it together from fantasy, things that existed only in my head and while this is still a work of fiction, this book seemed to meld into my reality.

Coming towards the end of this book, much like the characters in this book, my life started falling to pieces so much so that this book almost didn't make it to being published.

Every emotion from the main female character in this book is an emotion I felt while writing this book. I think on some level I wrote her that way because in some respects she is me.

At the time of publishing this piece, I felt lost and hopeless and my only salvation was I could write something to see me through the dark parts of what had become to seem like hopelessness.

Ava was the light to his dark and I think that in the dark light must shine through so we can make it to the other side.

Darkness also brings with it lessons and growth and even though we can't see it while it is happening. Sometimes, maybe sometimes, we need to sit alone in the dark to appreciate the light.

Calia xoxo

PART ONE

I have a perfect life.
A life that most would
kill for.
I worked hard for
this.
Little did I know the
girl who used to hunt,
would be the one
getting hunted.

AVA

1

THE JOB

THE GHOST

The photograph in my hands causes a crease to form at my brow. I knew this girl. She had betrayed me a long time ago, and I had just let her get away. It was akin to poetic justice. Her life was in the palm of my hands. I clench the photograph in my hand. And I was going to crush it.

Ava Valentina.

Even the thought of her name leaves a foul taste in my mouth.

Although I had let her go, the memory of that pesky little vixen lingered in my mind for ten years. Then, chance came knocking when someone recognized her in my town.

She should have stayed out of sight, because now she is within my reach.

Escaping won't be so easy for her this time.

Karma was on its way, bringing with it everything little Ava deserved.

I have a clear view of Ava in her kitchen from the woodland trees. She was making this too easy for me. The picturesque dwelling she had chosen had given me the perfect spot to watch her.

I had thought it would have been much harder, but she was making this too easy. I glance at her face, still as stunning as before, but what was I hoping for? Wasn't that what had caught my attention in the beginning?

The flowing of her long golden hair accompanies each movement her body makes. She throws back another beer and laughs with her guests. The sway of her hips ignites an unwarranted desire within me.

Everything about Ava drew you in. Her scent. Her smile. When she smiled, her dimples would create a striking contrast against her creamy complexion. Not one of those fake smiles, but a genuine one that lights up your face and makes your eyes dance. Speaking of her eyes, goddamn, she had the most majestic, iciest blue eyes I'd ever seen. So much depth, so many secrets.

The thought of those captivating eyes and tempting mouth causes my jaw to clench. She disappears into the night, taking my bank balance with her. She not only drained my balls that night, but also drained my account.

I was in for a shock when I woke up the next morning and discovered she had disappeared. The image of her body etched itself into my mind. I didn't know how she got under my skin, but she did.

That night, I wasn't even supposed to be out. I always enjoyed a drink and a good fuck after a kill.

"Now, how did you ever think you could escape me?" I taunt tonight's unwilling victim.

Victor Rossi, a bastard by nature. Finding him was a breeze, but seeing what he was up to, well, that just made my blood boil. Victor was notorious for trafficking women, women. This girl, who couldn't have been over fourteen, was at this terrible den when I got there.

It filled the air with the stench of blood, sweat, and sex. I would have embraced the scent, one of my three favorite things in life. However, when I see her bruised and bloody body on the floor, I am filled with nothing but repulsion.

He waves his cock above her motionless body, swaying his hips as he sprays piss over her slight frame. Anger flows through me like madness through the disturbed.

As he enjoys his moment of bliss, he remains oblivious to my silent approach from behind. I feel his body tense up as my hand grips the back of his neck. "I knew you were a bastard, Rossi, but kids?" Against his neck, I let out a fierce snarl.

He remains silent. Fortunately, I would prefer not to have to remove his tongue earlier than intended. The sounds of torture and death would create a melodic serenade.

"Now, what will we do with you?" I mock.

"Please, please let me free." He begs, begging me? Like a little lost boy.

I couldn't believe that the once feared member of New York's most notorious gang now appeared as a pathetic miscreant. The drool hung from his mouth while fear pierced his black eyes. He was unmissable, like staring into the abyss, devoid of soul.

My intention was to have fun before doing the world a favour.

"Please, please let me go." He begs once more.

"Why would I do that?" I smirk, "when we are having so much fun."

"Let me go, you crazy bastard." He spits at me.

"Ah, that's more like it." I crack my knuckles after I throw him to the ground. "My mother used to tell me to never play with my food, but you know what?" He shakes his head as he scrambles on his hands and knees trying to move away from me. "It's more fun when your food thinks it can get away."

He scrambles to get on his feet and begins running.

The chase was on.

"Run, food, run." I scream as I stroll in the same direction he's just ran in.

This was the part I relished. Adrenaline pulsed in my veins. He accepted his fate, yet a glimmer of hope remained that he could escape. Be the first to outwit me.

I walk at a steady pace, my ears tuned to any signs of life. The thrill of the hunt fills me as I detect the vermin I'm about to eliminate. That he could outsmart me brought a chuckle to my throat.

Entering a room devoid of light, filled with death and decay. The only thing audible is the rhythmic tapping of my shoes on the concrete floor.

I'm close.

So close.

It filled the air with the noxious smell of vermin.

I am enveloped by the sound of his raspy breath.

I pause at the exact spot where I suspect something concealed him while closing in on the breathing. Looking around, I pause. "Guess the bastard outsmarted me," I sigh. Listening to the ragged breathing slow to relief.

I wait.

I can detect the sound of his feet scuffling across the concrete floor. The only question was whether the little piggy would come out or if I would need to bring him out.

Once more, I wait. Although I'm a patient person, the anticipation drives me insane. Oh, so sweet would be the reward for ending his life! Despite the scuffing of his feet, he does not make a move to reappear. Kicking and squealing it is, I think with a smile.

Reaching down, my hand rests on the back of his neck and I hear the slow gasp of surprise. "You lose, little piggy." While pulling his body across the floor and staring down at him with disgust. "Rossi, I must confess, I'm disappointed."

"Listen—." His eyes are pleading with me. Oh, he wants to make a deal. This should be interesting.

"Go ahead."

He looks surprised.

"Sure, why not?" I smile. "You explain to me why I should let you go and maybe I will be generous and let you live today," I smirk.

"You know who I work for, right?" Oh, and disappointment hits me again. I lacked a fucking better nature, which he failed to realize. Idiot.

"I do." I smile, "You also should know by now that I don't care who you work for."

"Nikoli will rip you to pieces." He screams.

I smile. "I'm looking forward to seeing that." My foot stamps hard against his ribs and the cracking of his bones is like music to my ears. "Come on, Rossi, you know your little posse doesn't scare me."

"No," He wheezes through the pain that I imagine is attacking his body. "well that's very idiotic. Nikoli will—." Once more my boot crashes down, this time connecting with his face. Blood seeps from the side of his snarling mouth. "Nikoli will—." My fist connects with his head, his head moves to the side and he lies motionless, just like that fucking girl he had defiled.

It wasn't a difficult feat to fasten his body to the chains. Gripping the thick links, I exert force to pull. Witnessing his body soar to great heights. Only his head slumps as I fasten the chain around the bollards. The crazy bastard wasn't going anywhere.

As I hold a bucket of freezing water, I grin while launching the icy contents at his head. His head lifts and his icy gaze meets mine, accompanied by a loud gasp. "Welcome back, Princess," I smirk.

He assesses his surroundings as his head moves across the room, a look of confusion appearing on his face. "Why am I up here?" He screams. "Let me down."

A smile pinches through my mouth. "Well, you looked uncomfortable slumped on the ground. I'm nothing if I'm not accommodating. Wouldn't want your boss to think I didn't give you the five-star service, now would I?"

"You'll hang for this." He grits at me.

"I'm not the one hanging." I wink. "Our time together is almost over. It has been fun and I will always remember you as my little screamer." I pinch his cheek and watch as he whips his head away from my touch.

The sight of the wood gathered beneath his feet brings a smirk to my lips. The silver lighter in my pocket brushed against my hand. In one motion, I fling it into the air and then catch it. "Did you know the best way to get rid of a virus?" He looks at me with a crease forming on his brow. "No? I have discovered that the best way to eradicate a virus is through burning. And you Rossi are a virus," I smirk.

Above the roaring fire, his feet sway. Smoke from the flames is already in the air. "Let me down." He screams.

Using the chains, I bring him down towards the flames, positioning his feet above the fire. His screams cut through the air. "Like I said, I'm accommodating."

"No, no, no." He screams, "It's hot. It's boiling."

"Is it?" I cock a brow. "I can't feel anything."

"It's hot. Please, please make it stop." He screams with tears in his eyes. "Let me down." He screams once more.

"As you wish," I smirk, once again pulling him down onto the flames and dipping his feet into the flames. His screams resonate as the flames consume him. "You wanted to come down and down you will come."

Lowering his body, I hear his screams. Nowhere in the world will you hear a sound like this. It's as if they always sense the impending end, and his body becomes engulfed in flames, resulting in the scorching of his charred skin. My lips curl into a smile. Today, I've contributed to the world.

The only way to eradicate a virus is through burning, and I hear its agonizing screams as death nears its repulsive form. I would expel the virus, leaving only charcoal and ash in his body.

The cleanup crew would handle the remaining tasks. You could smell the stench of his charred flesh, and it was a delicacy I would give to him. Thumbing a text to the clean-up crew:

Clean up on aisle three

I placed my phone back in my pocket and sighed. There was

only one last task remaining. Despite the joy of burning that prick, this always reminded me of my humanity. It fractured the remnants of my heart within my hollow chest.

The only sound that echoed through the damp and desolate warehouse as I walked back was the pounding of my feet and my breathing. My heart raced. Hurting someone never matched the intensity I felt during the last step. Taking a life was easy, but this was pure agony.

She shows no sign of movement, standing right in front of her. It was not possible for her to have survived an attack like that. When Gage asked me why I returned to them after killing their abuser, my response was straightforward: wouldn't you want to know what happened to your child if they vanished without a trace? I felt it was my duty to bring their babies home and say a last goodbye.

I can't help but grimace as I kneel next to her motionless body. What makes men attracted to something so innocent? Disgusting. My lips release a sigh. "Poor thing. How did you end up here?" I mutter. Looking down, her complexion was ghastly pale and her hair was raven black and matted. So innocent. So young. Such a waste.

Feeling her neck, her skin is clammy and cold, but then I widen my eyes. "Well, aren't you a little fighter?" I smile. I couldn't believe it. She was still alive. Warmth flooded my body as my mouth opened, replacing the pain.

I lift her weak body and cover her with my jacket, preserving her dignity. As they rush her through the doors on the bed, I feel relief after dropping her off at the hospital. "Sir, do you want your coat back?" The nurse asks.

"No, let her keep it." I smile.

"Wait, what is your—."

I could sense that she was about to inquire about my name. They always asked that, but I had already vanished into the shadows, observing her confusion at my sudden disappearance. It wasn't always like this. They would go home in a box, but today brought a happy ending to an awful day.

I need a drink. I reckon I had deserved that much, or at least I believe so, as I walk down the lit street and step into my cherished sleazy bar.

"Welcome home," I mutter as I walk through the doors of the **BLACK DIAMOND.**

THE GHOST

TEN YEARS AGO

My body was coursing with adrenaline after the last job. Even as he took his last breath, the screams continued to echo in my ear. It was as if music filled my ears, but the excitement only arose when their breath halted and there was only silence around me.

A clean shirt and a few Jack Daniels later, I'm feeling more relaxed. The echoing music surrounds me, but I pay no attention. The blood-lust following the last kill has only just dispersed. Even the erotic dancers on stage cannot hold my attention.

I wasn't sure what was wrong with me. **BLACK DIAMOND** was a notorious hang-out for the dregs of society. Those doors wouldn't catch the attention of any high-class individuals. Mobsters, thieves, crooks, murderers. If you were on the wrong side of life, this was the go-to spot. Despite its deceptive appearance. From an insider's point of view, this appeared to be the epitome of style.

It felt like a tiny demon, luring you into a false sense of safety, gripping you with its claws, and tempting you to indulge in your deepest, darkest wishes. My desires peaked as she glided across the room, like an angel I can't look away from. Was I drooling? I run my hand across my face, searching for drool, but breathe a sigh of relief when I find it's dry.

Her legs come my way, her enticing hips swaying, tempting me like a seductive seductress. She didn't even notice me, but she caught my attention, which hasn't been easy. I can't help but feel desire curling inside me when I see her move. Her presence compelled me to pause, shrouded in her spell. Her hair, a vibrant golden hue like the sun, flows down her body in waves, making her irresistible the closer she gets.

"Mind if I join you? Her enchanting voice seduces my senses. Not only was she angelic in appearance, but she also had an angelic voice. I just nod and watch as she moves her perfect ass onto the seat next to me. "Not much of a talker?" She smiles.

"Depends on the conversation." Her plump pink lips press together as if she's deep in thought.

"I'm Ava, by the way." She smiles while holding out her small, delicate hand. I scoff as I feel the juxtaposition of her supple skin against the roughness in my palm while holding her hand. "Do you have a name?"

"Doesn't everyone have a name?" I smirk, "still deciding if I want to give that."

"Hostile," she smiles, "I like it." My brows shift in confusion. "No names. How about you buy me a drink instead?" This girl had brass balls, I had to give her that.

"Sure, why not?" I smirk. "What will it be?"

"I will have what you're having. What is it? Scotch? She asks.

"Not quite," I smirk. "Two more." I signal the bartender to bring a fresh round of drinks. He nods, and before I can react, two more drinks are forcefully placed in front of us.

"So, nameless stranger." She brings the glass to her lips and I smirk as I see a grimace cross her plump lips. "What's your story?" Oh, great, we were going to have a pleasant conversation. I just sit there pursing my lips, thinking if I want to divulge any information to the surprise that sits before me. "Not much of a talker, uh, oh well, I can talk and you can listen." She states as she swallows the last dregs of the whiskey from the glass.

"Bold of you to assume I want to listen to you," I smirk while my eyes run across her silky fucking legs I can't stop imagining draped across my shoulders.

"Ouch," her hands clasped across her heart. "Hit me where it hurts." A small chuckle squeezes from my throat. "Wow, is that a laugh?"

"No," I shake my head at her. "That was not a laugh."

"No?" She raises a brow. "kind of sounded like a laugh and dare I say a smile." She grins. "You should do that more."

"Do what?"

"Smile," I watch as her fingers tease the rim of the glass. Every movement she makes doesn't go unnoticed. "I mean, I dig this whole brooding act of yours but—." Her fingers shift to her hair. "You have a pretty smile." She mutters.

I'm bewildered as I lock eyes with her, but soon I'm taken aback in surprise. Fuck. Was she blushing? The blush on her creamy complexion travels from her slender neck to her cheeks, eliciting an immediate response in my body.

"You going shy on me now?" I whisper.

"Uh, no—I," she struggles to get her words out.

"Oh, you are shy, baby." The moment those words leave my lips, her eyes widen and that blush grows into a beautiful pink blush. Fuck, I had never been this hard in my life.

"I still don't know your name." She smiles.

"Why do you want to know my name?"

"Well," her fingers tease my bare arms, and I shudder in response. "I want to know what name to call out when you fuck me." She whispers.

"Oh baby, you won't need a name for that," I smirk.

"Why not?" She pouts.

"Why don't I walk you home?"

"Oh, okay." I watch her face fall and I should do as I've told her I'm going to do. I should take her home. That's where she should be, not with me, but I can't help fantasizing about how her perfect little body would feel against mine.

The girl I had just met, who was happy and talkative, became quiet when we went outside. She refused to make eye contact with me. Maybe she didn't do this often, but I could feel the tension between us. I wasn't sure if that was a good thing or not.

I passed by the small Chinese lady who always stood on this street corner. I get an idea as I gaze upon the different flower arrangements on the table, sheltered from the rain by the tent.

"What is your favourite flower?" I whisper into her ear.

"My what?" Her eyes widen.

"Your favourite flower," I repeat.

"Oh, nobody has ever asked me that before." Her lips tighten together. "Red roses." She answers.

"Wait here," I instructed her, unsure if she was just going to flee into the night because this was strange, even by my standards.

As I approach her, she looks like an angel standing in the rain. "Close your eyes," she does as I ask, with no questions asked. Too trusting. I move my hand from my back and place the single red rose into her hands. "Now, open them."

Her eyes open and she glances down at the Rose cradled in her palms. I hear a gasp pass her lips, "You bought me a flower," her eyes are wide with wonder as they etch up my body until her eyes are looking into mine and everything stops. Everything in the world stands still. There is nothing, just me and her. "Nobody has ever given me anything." She chokes back a sob.

How was that possible? Was she unaware of her own presence? How could it be that anyone had never given her anything? She's on the verge of tears, her eyes revealing the truth; something as simple as a flower can make her cry. I didn't find many things surprising, but she was an exception.

She smiles—a smile I never saw coming. "Thank you," I hear

her utter. I can't remember a single time someone appreciated something I did in this god-forsaken place called life. Now I'm the one who's shocked. Great, the little vixen was getting under my skin, but I just wanted to fuck her, didn't I?

"I thought you were walking me home." She asks after light-years of silence.

"Is that what I said?" I smirk and she responds with a gentle nod. "Well, I walked you to my home." I smile. Her face falls as her eyes move across my estate. "If you are uncomfortable, I can still take you home."

"No," she shakes her head. "This—this is fine."

"Don't look so worried—I don't bite, well, not unless you want me to." I wink.

Her entire demeanor reflects that of a timid and shy girl. I can't understand it - she wouldn't stop talking in the bar, but now she looks like she's about to bolt in the opposite direction.

Once we are inside, I hear a sigh pass her lips. "Shall we get it over with, then?"

"Get it over with? Get what over with?" I smirk.

"Uh," she shifts from one foot to the other. "You know." She whispers.

"I'm afraid I don't. If you don't want to do anything, we won't. I am not forcing you to do anything you don't want to do. So, please can you come sit down? You are making me nervous." I smile.

The timid little thing walks towards me. The cream and gold stone floor resounds with the clangs of her heels with each step. I placed her little body next to mine, but she's still not close enough. The moment she's near me, the scent of sweetness overwhelmed my senses. While I bring her body close to mine, she tenses until my fingers glide along her arms, melting her tension away, allowing her to release a contented sigh.

"See, that's better," I whisper into her hair.

"Why are you been so nice to me?"

"Why wouldn't I be nice, Ava? Have you done anything to cause me to want to be mean?" She shakes her head. "Well, stop asking me silly questions, silly girl."

Her skin feels smooth beneath my hands and desire consumes me. My breath quickens as soon as my fingers contact her soft, little body. She remains oblivious to my intense desire for her. Her touch awakens something untamed deep within me.

My fingers caress her body, moving downwards. Hitting her thighs and Christ, they feel just as fucking good, if not better. I just want to open her legs and bury myself within her. I run my fingers along her thighs, causing her body to jolt and shudder. I can't tell if it's fear or excitement anymore.

My fingers caress her inner thighs, eliciting a long, soft moan from her. Oh, and it's the sweetest fucking sound I've ever heard, "please," she begs, "please touch me."

"Such an eager little thing," I smirk. Tipping my head towards hers, I kiss her, devouring her as if she's my last meal, relishing the taste of her strawberry lip gloss as my tongue delves into the depths of her mouth. I'm on the verge of losing control, my heart pounding with excitement like hers against my chest.

"Please," I hear her utter in my mouth. God, she sounded fucking sexy when she begged.

As my fingers explore her neck, she gasps and our lips collide. Her body ignites with the slightest touch. Each slow movement of my fingers leaves her breathless. My desperate little slut. Shit, no. She wasn't mine—well, not yet, at least.

I kiss her neck, inhaling the delightful fragrance of her skin. She's like a forbidden flower, tempting me to open up and devour. "Spread your legs," I whisper into her skin. She remains motionless, only uttering whimpers. Oh, the poor little puppy can't even follow a simple instruction. I meet her gaze as she lifts her head. "I said spread your fucking legs." A moan crawls from her throat. "Oh, baby, if you want to cum, you'll spread those gorgeous fucking legs of yours." My hands slide up her thighs. "Or I can always make you spread them." I watch as her eyes widen.

"Make me?" She gasps.

"Poor little baby," another moan. God, she was fucking tormenting me. My hands trace up her thighs, my body spinning as I kneel before her, treating her like my fucking queen. Shit, not yet — not yet.

As I dig my fingers into her skin, I raise my eyes and find her staring down at me with uncertainty and a slight blush on her cheeks, causing her to gasp. "Spread your legs," I growl. Her legs stay still and a little smirk appears on those cock teasing lips. "Fine, darling, the hard way it is." Digging my fingers deeper into her skin, a tiny moan crawls from her throat as I spread her legs open. "See how easy that was?" I smirk.

Drawing myself nearer and gathering her dress around her waist, she lies there, observing me. She stays still, allowing me to do whatever I want. Within her enchanting blue eyes, there is a feverish desire as she watches. I use my teeth to remove her lacy black thong and uncover her wet desire.

"Spread them wider," I instruct with impatience running through my tone.

"You're very bossy, has anyone—." My hand grips her throat, tightening until I hear her gasp.

"I said spread your fucking legs," I growl down her ear and just like magic, I hear the deep pleasurable moan and she spreads wide her legs for me to devour her. "Good Girl," I praise her.

Lowering my head to the space between her thighs, I glide my nose against her soaked opening, inhaling her scent. "Fuck, you smell fucking delicious," her body shudders in response to my words. "I can't wait to fucking taste you." My fingers grip her thighs and I move her body towards mine and just take a moment to look at her.

The sight of her pussy glistening with her own juices is perfect. Hunger drives my tongue across my lips as I catch her intense gaze, slipping her a small smirk before diving back between her beautiful legs. The anticipation of what comes next has her body trembling, making mine shiver with excitement.

As I glide my tongue across her lips, damn, she tastes just as sweet as she smells. My god! I use my hands to widen the gap between her legs, longing to bury my face in her irresistible pussy. I flick my tongue out with quick, gentle strokes, clamping my lips against hers. "Oh god, oh god, oh my fucking god." She screams almost instantly.

I indulge in her like a desperate feast, feeling her shudder with pleasure under my passionate caress.

Her hands come down onto my head, her nails piercing my skull and driving my face deeper into her pussy. My god, she's fucking delicious. I could eat her pussy all night long, but I couldn't wait to feel how amazing her pussy felt wrapped around my cock.

While preparing to enter her, I remove my tongue and she whimpers. Such a desperate little whore, begging to be filled. That thought alone made me ache with desire.

I enjoy the flavor of her as my tongue glides up her lips, savoring every drop. With my fingers curled and inside her, she screams right away as I move my hand faster and deeper within her wet pussy.

As she gets closer, her screams are now incoherent. Almost ready, her eyes glaze over and her body shakes. Her pussy tightens around my fingers, and her screams are now muffled, like she's struggling for breath.

"Come on, baby, relax." Her head shakes. "it's okay, you can do it." I coo at her.

"It's too much," she shakes her head once more. "It's too much." Tears are streaming down her face now. God, does she know how sexy she looks when she cries? "I can't," she cries once more.

"Oh you can," I smirk. "And you will." My fingers curl deeper inside of her and a loud piercing scream squeezes from her throat. "That's right baby, let go," I gasp as the juices squirt from her pulsing pussy. Her juice covering my face. I want to be consumed by her essence. As my tongue slithers out across my lips, I taste her again. "Such a good girl," I rasp. "Look at the mess you made," her eyes widen, "I'm so proud of you, now taste yourself." I don't give her a chance to refuse. My lips mash against hers and my tongue wrestles with hers and moans fall into my mouth as we both bask in her juices that cover us.

"What—what was that?" She asks me.

"What was what?" I smirk.

"That—that was different,"

"Different good or different bad?"

"I—I don't know." She stammers out.

"Well, did you enjoy it?" She nods, "then you have your answer," I whisper.

I stand, extending my hand, but she seems unsure of what to do with it. "The way it works is, you take my hand in yours. It's quite simple."

"I'm not sure I can move—after that."

"Well, you are in a world of trouble, little lady," leaning down and placing my hands beneath her ass, I hoist her in the air and pull her body close to mine. "Because I'm not done with you yet."

As her arms coil around my neck, a troubling thought arises in my mind. As I held her, her body molded against mine, but it was too close, too soon to feel anything for a girl I had just met.

"Where are you taking me?" She asks.

"Where you belong—in my bed."

She remains quiet as I climb the stairs with her in my arms. Her body's warmth and snugness against mine make me want to hold on tight. I want to keep her in my arms forever. Shit, how had she crawled under my skin so fast? When I brought a girl back I couldn't wait to be rid of them. They were a temporary pleasure, but Ava—Ava was in a league of her own. I longed for something I had never longed for. I wanted to keep her.

Impatience causes me to open the door by shouldering it. The feel of her against me has my mind wondering how her pussy will feel around my cock, feeling her make a mess of me as the tingling of desire crawling up and down my spine.

Throwing her onto the bed, she lets out a cute little squeal and my God does my cock jump in response. Crawling on the bed, she's trapped beneath my body, but there is no fear, no shyness, just desire swirling within her eyes as she looks up at me. "Now, what are you going to do with me? Now you've got me here?" She taunts.

"Open your mouth," Her mouth gaped open and holding the spit from my mouth she looked unsure but she still lay still with her mouth open wide and her tongue hanging out, waiting for her treat. The spit falls from my mouth and into hers. I watch her eyes widen as it hits her tongue. "Good little slut." My mouth crashes down against hers in a melding of fierce desire wrapped between our eager mouths that wrestles to devour one another.

My hands tear off her dress, revealing her enticing curves that could tempt any man nearby. Her voluptuous perfect tits bounce, free from the tight figure-hugging dress that had tempted me to want this spectacular vision I saw before me and now she is bare, soaking and fucking ready for me. "Don't move," I instruct. Oddly, I felt annoyed that I had to move away from her body.

When I came back, she was lying motionless in the room, just as I had left her. Consistently adhering to my instructions without deviation, she proved to be an exceptional student. Tonight, she was going to receive everything she deserved—and I meant everything. With a silver bucket in hand, I position it near the bed before crawling over her flawless body, becoming aroused.

Reaching down, I pull out an ice cube from the bucket and hold it between my teeth. A crease forms at her brow. "What's that for? I choose not to respond and instead give her a tight smile, dragging the ice cube over her already peaked nipple. "Oh fuck," she cries out. Running the ice cube in circles, pimples rise across her chest. "Oh god, that feels—so fucking good." She gasps. I observe her breath becoming erratic as I glide the ice cube over her body, feeling the coldness sinking into her skin. Sliding down and melting from her body heat, it settled in her belly button. I watch the water drip down her perfect little body, dripping onto her glistening pussy.

As I take another ice cube in my mouth, I trace it up her inner thighs, her body trembling underneath me while plea-sure-filled gasps echo in the air. moving the cube towards her throbbing wetness, wrapping it around her sensitive clit, the soft gasps escalate into intense screams. "Please, oh god—fuck," she screams. The taste of her lingers on my lips as I slide it up and down her pussy lips again.

I can't believe how incredibly sweet she tastes. I slide the ice cube down and spread her open, slipping it inside before sucking it back into my mouth. Her lips release sharp gasps of desire every time the cube enters her. I press my lips against her dripping hole, slipping the ice cube into her wet pussy and swirling it with my tongue. "Oh god, oh god—oh fuck." I hear her scream her release as I feel the warm desire pour out of her and into my mouth.

Sliding up her body, I grip her wrists and hold them above her head, restraining her from moving. "Now you're ready, baby."

Her eyes widen. "ready for what?" she gasps.

"Ready for me," I smirk, sliding between her legs and placing my throbbing cock at her centre. Fuck. She's so tight. Despite my slow movements, I have yet to enter her tight, sweet pussy. "Just relax for me, baby." I plead.

I push through and her pussy grips me, like she's strangling me. "oh fuck," I gasp as soon as I enter her. "Fuck, baby, you feel so fucking good." I gasp. I take my time, savoring every sensation as her pussy dances against my cock. Desire fuels never-ending bursts of pleasure filling my spine.

As I let go of her arms, I grab her by the throat and thrust into her tight pussy. "Oh fuck, oh god, oh my god." She screams every time I spear my cock deep within her dripping cunt. The way her body melts against mine has the grip around her throat tightening. Each time I squeeze harder, she grips my cock around her tight pulsing pussy and I have to fight to not release all the desire that I need to pour into her.

"That's good. You're so fucking good for me." I gasp. I will not last much longer. My cock moves deeper within her and her screams pierce my eardrums. It's like music to my fucking ears. "That's—it—baby; cum; for; me," I rasp. Craving my release, I twirl my hips and penetrate her, sensing her body tremble with undulating desire. I feel her wetness coating me. I'm fucking soaked. "Fuck," I cry out, feeling the strands of my desire fall into her perfect dripping hole.

Her cum covers my cock when I pull my cock out of her and sweat slides down every part of my body. I fall beside her, breathless and covered in sweat. "Fuck, you are such a good little slut." I rasp.

Her eyes, glazed over with lust, looked pretty as she looked at me. Her eyes were already beautiful, but now they were even more captivating, and her flushed face looked perfect, resembling a cute little doll. She looked perfect when she got fucked.

Sliding my arms across her body, I pull her close. "What are you doing?" She stammers.

"We are going to sleep."

"Like this?"

"Yes, now close your eyes."

"But, I'm not tired." She whines.

"Silly girl, sleep."

In just a few moments, I am comforted by the sound of her peaceful slumber, and my body eases. Wrapped in her warm embrace, I let my eyes close and feel content with this surprise lying in my arms.

3

LITTLE BEAST

THE GHOST

I should've just walked in there. Let her know I found her, revealing my true self after all this time. I wanted her to realize that no matter the distance, she could never escape her past—she could never escape me.

While looking at her from the trees, I can't bring myself to do it. Grant her an easy way out when she came face to face with the ghost she had forgotten about. No, when Ava saw me I wanted to see her face pale in comparison with the realisation that she would never be free. Her past had caught up to her, and now the ghost was here to collect.

I monitor her every move. She remains oblivious to the fact that I have been watching her. Moving through her mundane tasks of the day, unaware that in the forest just next to her house lies something she never thought she would see again. I get an odd satisfaction watching her. The sliver of excitement pierces my spine. She is oblivious to my presence. Ava is oblivious to the ghost who lurks in the shadows.

The curtains remain drawn and it shrouded her house in darkness. Damn it! Now I could not witness what the little beast was up to. The light upstairs stays on for hours, my boots scuff across the mud and the leaves. Fall was in full swing and the wind was peaking to icy, but the stings of pain that lashed across my face were the only sensation that let me know I was still human.

The light turns off, and the house is a black abyss. A smile falls across my lips. Ah, the little beast must have gone to sleep. In a peaceful slumber with not a care in the world. Bleeding men dry one at a time. My jaw ticks as I think of that little beast roaming from man to man. Well, those days were in the past. The little beast wouldn't betray another man because the one she deceived was back, and it was time for her to face the consequences.

I am aware of my boot crushing under the leaves beneath my feet as I exit the forest. Came out of my hiding place. It appeared they had camouflaged me among the trees for months and now I was reemerging during the stillness of the night. Ava lived in a place without neighbors, which was almost too perfect—no witnesses.

While traversing the stone steps, the small creature spared no expense obscuring this property. I pondered on the count of men she had been involved with obtaining a piece of land like this. My hand touches the handle. When I pull it downwards, I realize it is in a locked position. So, she wasn't stupid after all. I was hoping she had not yet installed an alarm system. Or it was back in the forest for me.

Withdrawing the lock-pick knife from my pocket, I align it correctly, manipulating the lock until I perceive the click. A smile spreads across my face when I pull down that handle and swing open the door. I waited for the loud alarm to give her a warning that there was an intruder in her house, but to my surprise, there was nothing. Nothing but the sweet sound of silence.

My feet move into her house. The house that is shrouded in darkness. Moving around, I take in my surroundings. I roll my eyes at the pretentiousness of her show home in the woods. Christ, it doesn't even look lived in. Cared more about appearances than living life. Well, she would witness her hopeful, pretentious dreams shattered.

I would take in my surroundings and investigate the target. Familiarize myself with all the information about the mark, but I was already well-informed about Ava. She was a con artist who eluded my grasp, but she made a mistake. She let down her guard, resulting in my men finding her.

I creep up the winding staircase. As pretentious as her show home was, the architecture was beautiful. No wonder she stayed and didn't leave her house. I'm not sure I would either if I had everything at my ass. What would she need to leave for?

Her bedroom door is ajar, with nothing but a tiny stream of light guiding the way into her bedroom. A crease forms across my brow. Ava scared of the dark? That made little sense. Little beast feared nothing. sliding my hand over the cream and gold door. It moves with ease, with no creaking in sight. The only thing that reaches my ears is the sound of her soft, deep breathing. She is unaware of someone's presence in the room with her.

As I move closer to her bed, I stand there, towering above her. Directing great intensity towards her relaxed body. Unaware that her enemy watched her while she slept. I possess the ability to exact my revenge. It would be so easy, so why did I sense frustration over not being able to glimpse her enchanting eyes?

Her hair falls across her face in a mass of golden light, like sunlight seeped from her poisonous veins. She proved to be the most terrible type of enemy I ever encountered by chance. This one didn't hide her ugly on the outside. She lured you in like a siren, luring men to their deaths. No, Ava didn't conceal the ugliness of her true nature because her ugliness lived in a place beyond visibility, buried within her where it would remain unseen—only if you ventured near.

I believed I was close. I resisted the temptation to let her in, not extensively, but more than I did for any other person. It wasn't her fault. That was my mistake. I realized she was trouble as soon as my eyes caught sight of that sweet body of hers. Her baby blue eyes were full of innocence and yet something deeper. Unbeknownst to me, there was a sinister agenda lurking behind those sapphire gems.

Now, as I gaze upon her tranquil sleep, rage builds up within me, but as I lean nearer, moving her soft golden strands aside, I perceive something else. It's not rage, it's something un-welcome. Desire mixed with a need to protect this poisonous beauty. Yes, Ava needed protection. Not from some outside enemy she needed protection from—me.

My fingers slide across the silky skin on her face, a small con-tented sigh falls from her lips and I am still, unaware if her eyes will snap open and she will come face to face with the enemy she had evaded for all these years but she stays still in her peaceful slumber.

My lips brush her skin and it's like I'm coveted in her warm embrace once more, but I know that every moment with Ava was a lie. Even if it was a lie, I wanted to go back to that lie–even for just one second. It was the only time I ever felt like I was here, that I existed, even if it was a lie—I needed it.

The touch of her skin on my lips evokes that same emotion, the emotion that only Ava had the power to evoke in me. I close my eyes and allow my breath to dance across her skin. "You may be a little beast, but you have always been my little beast," I whisper against her skin.

Sighing, I pull myself away from her and place a gift on the nightstand, smirking. I'm interested to know if she will know who came to visit her during the night while she sleeps.

Moving away from her, my shoulders droop. I wish it could be a different way without the effort of these games, but it couldn't—not with her. This was the only way it could be.

* * *

Walking away from the little beast left me feeling unfulfilled. What did I expect? Her to open her eyes and fall into my arms? That would not happen. In the unfortunate event that Ava had roused, a fight would occur. I wasn't oblivious to the fact that Ava may look sweet, but she had a fire that would encase you in the fires of hell.

So why was I playing with her? There's a chance that I simply had the urge to play with my food. Maybe I was playing with her because it's what she deserved. I wasn't sure why I was playing with her, but I hadn't felt this excited in years.

"Where the fuck have you been?" And just like that, my excitement dissipates.

"Damon, always a pleasure." I let a smirk play across my lips as I walked past him.

"Where are you going now?" He grits with annoyance. "Don't fucking walk away from me."

I can't help the smirk that once again pulls at my lips, "it's sweet that you missed me—." I fall into the chair by the roaring fire, stretching my neck. Man, it was rough on my body watching the beast from the woods, but I had seen her up close. Smelt her, almost tasted her.

Shit, what was I saying? I wanted revenge. Not.... not this.

"Oh, you're quite the comedian this morning." Damon mocks. "Where the fuck have you been?" I scowl at him. "Oh, please don't tell me—oh, of course, you're chasing a piece of ass while the shit collapses around us."

"I'm not chasing anything."

"No?" He cocks a brow. "So, you weren't with the mysterious girl in the woods?"

"Define with."

"Fuck, Chase, why don't you just fucking announce your

presence?" A crease forms across my brow. He was right, why didn't I? Why was I playing hunt my prey? "You know what? I don't care. We have a problem." He states in a dramatic tone.

My eyes rose, and I looked at the intensity swirling in the deep brown hues as he gazed back at me. He looks worried, but Damon never looks worried. He stands, not saying another word. His dark hair falls across his eyes, but that doesn't stop the frown of worry I can see laced within his eyes.

"You have my attention." I gasp, getting annoyed by the silence that ensues.

"You fucked up," I smirk. "Chase, you fucked up bad."

"Okay, I'll bite. What is it you think I did this time?"

"Nikoli has the entire city looking for you. There is a bounty on your head. What did you do?"

"You don't know?" I smirk.

"Why are you smiling, you crazy bastard? Did my words not reach your ears?"

"I heard you," I mutter as I stand.

"What did you do?" He grits once more.

"Took out the trash." I smile.

I watch as he brushes his fingers through his hair, the way he does when he's trying to control that rage that I know is running through his body. "Gage is pissed."

"Yeah?" I walk towards him, "so what else is new?"

"Chase," he calls after me, but I carry on walking. "Chase," he repeats once more.

"Don't worry about it."

"I will always remember to have that engraved on your tombstone."

Nikoli? Why was everyone afraid of Nikoli? I could end his shit in my sleep. A bounty on my head? That was an inconvenience. Watching Ava would be dangerous now, but I couldn't stop. What if she moved? I would never find her again. This was my only chance to get back at the little beast.

I would deal with Nikoli and his merry band of miscreants later, but right now there was only one thing on my mind:

Capturing Ava.

4

SECRET ADMIRER?

AVA

My eyes open and I sigh. Another day of doing what I considered was the dream. I put in a lot of effort for this. It was risky. He could find me at any moment. I knew that if he discovered me, he would once more confine me and condemn me to a lifetime of suffering under his dominance.

I couldn't go back.

I just wanted to forget, forget that he ever existed. Forget the torture he had committed me to, but I couldn't. Nightmares of our time together continued to haunt me. I was fortunate enough to get away from him. I wasn't sure I would be so lucky next time.

The sunlight hits my eyes as soon as they open. I had lived in the dark for so long that the only luxury I appreciated was light. It was my Saviour. After all, it was the only thing that had given me the understanding that I was still here, that I still existed and I wouldn't be clueless. Not again.

The buzzing from my phone jolts me from my thoughts. Reaching across, I pick up the phone, but my body freezes as my gaze falls upon my nightstand. I see a bunch of blood-red roses spread across my nightstand. The fear climbs from my body, pushing me deeper into an anxious pit of despair.

Somebody had placed these here while I slept.

They weren't there when I went to bed last night, but there they stood with a charcoal envelope wrapped in a blood-red ribbon. With shaky hands, I reach over, taking the envelope between my fingers and opening it to see an identical charcoal letter with gold lettering.

My eyes scan across the words and I'm unsure of my reactions as I read each word, becoming more and more puzzled.

Good morning, Ava

Have you ever realized how stunning you appear while you sleep? It's a pity because those blue eyes are something that has always enchanted me.

Suppose you're wondering how I crept around your house unnoticed.

Don't worry about that, little beast.

The truth will come to light.

But for now,

Enjoy your day.

Ghost.

The letter didn't instil calm in my body, quite the opposite. I throw the letter down, not even bothering to pick up the flowers. Let them die. I didn't care. How did he get in? Then the piercing fear hits me with one notion: he was here while I slept.

Then each notion would tumble across my already fried

brain.

Did I lock the door?

Was it someone I knew?

Someone from my past?

The man who gave me nightmares? I shiver at that thought alone. God, I hope not.

Little beast? Had he given me a nickname already? Can't say I enjoyed this one. It wasn't the most flattering.

The most important thought I had and the one that kept circling:

Who the fuck was Ghost?

I'm not sure how long I take to move out of my bed, but I trail my body down the stairs and sit in front of the steaming cup of coffee, staring into space. My morning had taken a horrendous turn. He was in my house. MY HOUSE.

"Where have you been?" I hear her screech as she crashes through the French doors. Jumping up, my heart rate flies to the moon. Looking across, I breathe a sigh of relief at my friend Audrey, who looks at me in confusion. "You're not dressed." She frowns.

"Thanks for stating the obvious," I smirk.

"You also haven't posted. What gives?"

"I'm allowed a day off." I sigh.

She clambers across to me, her long dark hair drapes across her body as she moves. Her big oval deep-set brown eyes peer at me with curiosity. Her hand moves across my forehead while she shakes her head.

"What are you doing?"

"Oh, you know, checking for sickness," I smirk. "You don't look sick." She shakes her head. "You're not hot." I shake my head at her theatrics. "So, that doesn't explain why you haven't posted." She takes a step back with her hands on her hips. "Well, I'm waiting. Now explain."

"Audrey Belvedere, you are impossible." I laugh.

"Ava, why haven't you posted?"

"I—." Picking up my hot cup of coffee, I blow across the liquid, allowing the steam to waft across my face. "Didn't feel like it," I mutter.

"You didn't feel like it?" A frown pierces her brow. "Ava, that doesn't sound like you. We worked hard to get where we are today. Nobody makes this kind of money working, but we did it." She slides onto the stool next to mine and places her hand across mine until I look at her. "What's going on?"

The words tumble out like verbal diarrhoea. "Has he found me?"

"What?" She shakes her head. "No, and he never will." My shoulders relax, "Why are you asking that? Why now?"

"I—I don't know, I'm being silly."

"Ava, I can't help you if you don't speak to me."

"It's nothing." I smile.

"Well, nothing has cost you a morning's work. Now tell me what's going on."

"Are you sure he hasn't found me?"

"Yes, your location is safe. We have hidden all your footprint data. He hasn't found you, I promise. You are like a ghost who disappeared from sight. You are safe."

Ghost? The moment those words leave her lips and my body shudders with fear. So, that's what he was doing, hiding in plain sight. It all made sense and yet, it made none.

"Well, someone has," I mutter.

"You're not making much sense." I hear Audrey sigh.

"I woke up and there were flowers and a note on my night-stand."

"That's sweet." She grimaces.

"Somebody put them there while I was asleep."

"Creepy." She now looks the way I do and now I don't feel like I've lost a sense of my sensibility because she's right. It is creepy. "I can fix this." She announces.

"You can?" I look at her with hope, like she holds all the

answers.

"Yeah, I know a guy." She puts her finger up to stop me from speaking and dials a number on her phone. Smiling, she waits for the elusive hero to pick up the phone. "Hey Chase, I need a favour." Well, that was an odd name, but if he could help me get back to a good night's rest, who was I to argue? I zone out and miss the rest of her conversation. "All done." She smiles.

"What's all done?"

"Chase will be by to install a security system, well, not him, but you get the drift."

"A security system?" My mouth gapes open. "Isn't that going a bit far?"

"Not at all. Your safety is what's important. You will sleep, get back to work and I won't have an aneurysm. Win, win." She smiles.

"Your the best, you know that."

"I know," she smiles. "So, how about we have a girly day?"

"You mean go out?" she nods. "Where there are people?"

"Yes, go out where there are people. You know it's not good

to be in this house all the time.”

“But I like my house. Where it’s safe and—.”

“I promise I wouldn’t put you at risk. Okay, forget the girly day. We should get you drunk.” She winks.

“Think I would rather see people than that.”

“It will be fun.” She laughs, “The worst thing that will happen is you might—.” She pulls my hair from my face. “Enjoy Yourself.” She whispers.

“Fine, what will we do until night falls?”

She presses a finger against her lips, “Well, I was thinking we could eat popcorn and watch movies.” My eyes widen. “Yes, I thought you’d agree to that.” She smiles.

The movie marathon was in full swing and I was enjoying myself. I had almost forgotten that there was a creep lurking around my house and invading my space while slept. The idea of a horror movie fest was my idea because what better way to scare yourself than to watch girls getting chased by psychos on the big screen?

"Are you sure you want to watch slasher movies?" Audrey asks.

"I know it might seem silly, given the circumstances, but it's not real. Isn't that the fun part of slasher movies, that you know it isn't real?"

"Why watch one when you're living one?" She jokes. My face drops. She wasn't wrong, though. "Hun, I was only joking."

"I know." I try to force a smile, but I can't even do that.

We both sit in silence as we watch a girl running on the big screen. I never got this part of the movie. I would often grimace at the screen. If we the viewers knew you shouldn't go in the room, why did the on-screen leading lady always walk towards the danger?

"If that was me, I would not be going into that room." I

gasped, while placing my hands across my face. "No, no, no, don't go in there," I scream at the stupidity of the girl running towards immediate death.

"Babe, it's not real." Audrey laughs.

"It's still painful to watch." I grimace and jump when the ominous music looms in the background. "Okay, if she would not die from stupidity, she's definitely going to die now."

"How do you figure that?"

"The music told me." I wink.

"You are crazy." She shakes her head, "Drink?"

"Sure," I smile. "No, don't open that door," I scream at the screen once more. The screams from the actress on the screen cause my body to jolt. "You don't even have a weapon. Why don't you have a weapon?" I once again speak my thoughts out loud as I watch the stupid leading lady walk into the killer's knife. "Sure, because we all walk towards a deadly weapon." I roll my eyes.

"What are you yelling at now?" I hear Audrey call from the kitchen.

Standing, I sigh. "Can you believe?—." I stand there stiff as I watch the shadow of a male cross the large bay window that overlooks the forest. Fear attacks my body and I can't breathe. The only words that strain my throat squeeze out in a hysterical screech. "He's here."

A breathless Audrey crashes back into the room, holding limes in her hand. "Who is here?" She breathlessly gasps.

"He—he—was at the window." I stutter as my body shakes and collapses to the ground.

The next thing I remember is blue lights flashing through my windows like a beam of hope. My body won't stop shaking. I can't even breathe. This day had been a nightmare, and something trapped me—I couldn't escape.

"We searched the perimeter and we couldn't find anything." The handsome police officer states.

"You hear that, babe? There is nobody out there. You are safe."

"But I saw him." I cry.

"Could you identify him?" The police officer asks me.

"Identify a shadow?"

"Then I'm afraid we can't do anything. If anything else happens, contact us."

"I could be dead by then," I whisper as tears crawl down my face, but he doesn't hear me. He's already closed the door and left before I even utter the dreadful words that have been spinning around my head all day.

"Ava,"

"He was there. He was, you believe me, don't you?"

"I believe you saw something, yes, babe, but he was right. You didn't see who it was, so who would they know to look for?"

"It's him, isn't it?" I sob.

"My dad? Skulking in the shadows." She shakes her head. "You know that's not his style."

"That's true. Then who is it?"

"I don't know." She whispers while stroking my hair on the floor. "You know what you need." I look up at her and shake my head. "Some heavy muscle." She smiles.

"Oh, yeah." I roll my eyes. "I keep that in my closet. Let me just go fish it out.”

“I know a guy.”

“No, Audrey.”

“Wouldn’t you feel safer with a bodyguard around here?”

“No, I would feel like I was being watched.”

“You already are. At least this way you would have somebody protecting you.”

“I don’t know.” I grimace at her idea of a bodyguard.

“Meet him. If you don’t like him, then we will just have to catch him on camera.” I peer at her closely. “I can see if he is available and he can watch you while we are out, as a kind of trial run. What do you think?”

“Okay,” I finally give in because what did I have to lose—only my life?

5

A JOB FOR CHASE

CHASE

How could she not remember me?

Was our night that unmemorable and the biggest question was, why did I fucking care? Only we knew what happened that night. The gift I left for her was supposed her make her realise. Why hadn't she figured out that her mystery guest was me?

The moment Audrey calls me, my blood is boiling. Some

guy? Some fucking guy and what had I done? Agreed to be her bodyguard. Well, it wasn't the worst idea I had ever had.

"Chase, are you coming?" Gage asks me.

"Sorry buddy, got a job to do."

"A job?" He raises a quizzical brow in my direction. "Hey Damon," I hear him shout. "Chase doesn't have a job scheduled, does he?" I groan as I see him striding towards us.

"Unless his job is to fuck something up, no." Ah, still annoyed about the whole being hunted by Nikoli.

"Then you're free?" Gage announces.

"No, I'm not. I have a job to do." I grit back.

"What job are you doing? Can I tag along?" Miles asks with a mouthful of chips. His long brown hair falls across his face and an innocent smile crosses his face as he looks back at me with his amber eyes full of mischief.

"No, I work alone."

"Come on, Chase, I'm bored." He whines.

"What's the job?" Damon interrupts.

"It's—," I run my fingers through my hair. "None of your goddamn business."

"Oh, please don't tell me, it's her."

"She needs a bodyguard," I smirk.

"From who?" He scowls at me. "Oh, you're a sick puppy."

"Don't start with me."

He lets out a roar of laughter. "I don't get the joke." Gage sighs.

"Oh, this sick bastard has been stalking Ava Valentina and if my calculations are correct, she now needs a bodyguard to protect her from none other than the bodyguard himself." He places his hands together and starts clapping.

"Don't fucking push me, Damon."

"Tell me, lover boy, what if the lady in question recognises you, then what?"

That was a brilliant question, but she didn't remember from the flowers I had given her, so there was every chance she would forget my face, right? A crease forms across my brow because did I want to take that chance. I wasn't ready to announce my arrival. Mine and Ava's fun had just begun, and I wasn't ready to show her I had found her.

"Cat got your tongue, Chase. I tell you what, I will go watch your sweet little project." The rage crawls through my body.

"Like fuck you will," I scream back at him.

"Careful now, Chase. Anyone would think you harboured feelings for the petty thief."

"The only feelings I have are sweet, sweet revenge," I smirk.

"Yeah," he smirks. "But that ass sure is a bonus, ay," he winks.

I must display the sliver of annoyance on my face because everyone but Damon scarpers from the room in moments like there is imminent danger and within moments everything in sight will be obliterated.

I don't even think as I rugby tackle him to the ground. My arms wrap around his neck, putting him in a chokehold, but the sick bastard looks up at me with a smile on his face. "If you wanted to cuddle, all you had to do was ask." His strained voice utters.

He digs his elbows into my ribs and a sharp gasp leaves my

throat as I try to breathe through the blow that penetrates my ribs. Once more he lands that blow in the same position and I release the hold I have on his neck, allowing him enough room to wriggle away from me.

He stands in a boxer's stance with his fists raised, still hungry for more, but he can't expect me to allow that slur to stand. jumping to my feet, I mimic his actions as I watch him dance backwards and forwards, readying himself to land the first blow.

"Stop them." Miles pleads with Gage.

"Why, I'm curious to see who wins," He smirks.

"Brothers shouldn't fight—not over a whore, anyway."

My head snaps towards Miles. "You want to be next?" He shakes his head. "Then keep your fucking opinions to yourself."

An outroar of laughter pours from Damon. "I have to say, for a man who only wants revenge, you sure are very—protective of the thief in question."

"Are you going to just stand there twinkle toes, or are you going to do something?" I mock.

"Twinkle toes?" He raises an amused brow. "You have got all the jokes today, Chase." He moves towards me. "If I didn't know any better, I would hazard a guess that your thief—" He sidesteps me with his hands raised. "Is making you soft," He whispers. A smirk falls across my lips as my fist connects with his face. I watch him stumble and wipe away the trickle of blood that slides down his nose. "Cheap shot." He screams as he once again moves towards me.

I don't even see the blow coming as he throws a punch with force straight to my gut. I'm winded. The breath crawls from my body and I stumble. Damon doesn't give me a chance to recover. He charges towards me, throwing both our bodies into the glass case that holds trophies. We both crash on the ground with the sound of glass clattering around us.

The loud bangs erupt as bullets fly through the walls and the ceilings, we both raise our heads.

"Pick this up another time." He smirks.

"Jackass." I mutter as we army crawl our way to safety.

"If I had to hazard a guess," Damon speaks, "I'd say Nikoli has found you." He smirks. "Now, are you going to tell me why you're on his hit list?"

"Does it matter?" A bullet flies straight towards us, missing Gage by an inch.

"I'd say it matters, yeah." Gage laughs. "What the fuck did you do, Chase?"

"Nothing much," I smile. "Just—killed one of his men."

"You did what?" Damon screams, "You better have a good reason for starting a fucking war with that crazy bastard!"

"I do."

"Well, we're waiting."

"Another time, we have more pressing issues at hand."

"Like what?"

"Oh, I don't know." I roll my eyes, "like staying alive."

I hear bangs as they try to enter the property. We only have a limited window before they all charge in here and take what they think is revenge for one dreg of society. I roll my eyes. Honestly, I did society a favour with that one.

By discreetly glancing around the door frame, I can determine if it's safe to proceed. They seemed to struggle. I would have been in the property by now. "Amateurs," I mutter.

"What's the plan?" Miles has parked himself up my ass, breathing down my neck.

"Wait." I grit back.

The sound of the shattering glass reaches my ears as something comes hurtling through the window. The ticking becomes audible to me as the dangerous device approaches. Our heads snap to the ticking bomb only a few feet from our bodies. "Move, now," I scream. We rush to the bedroom, which we had constructed for situations like this.

"Great, Chase, how are we supposed to escape from a room with no way out?" Gage screams.

A smirk crosses my lips. he had to give me more credit than that. Shoving the bed towards the wall, his eyes opened wide. "Shit, when did you have time to build this?" Pulling up the trap door, I watch as they climb down the stairs to the hidden tunnels beneath the house. Miles's head pops up. "This is genius. When did you do this?"

I shake my head, hearing the door fly off its hinges, "Ask questions later, move." I whisper. I smiled as the sound of the bed crashing back down on the ground reached my ears. With the right nudge, it would never stay up against the wall.

"Now what?" Damon asks.

"Now," I smile. "Now, we go home."

"Oh yeah, genius, tell me how we are going to do that when you have the entire city looking for you."

"Do you see anyone?" I smirk.

"Down here, no, only the rats," Gage mutters as he kicks a rat that scarpers into the steady stream of water that waves our way.

"Come on." I slap him on the back. "A big guy like you isn't scared of a little rat, right?"

"You know I don't like them." He grits back.

"Well, you better get used to them. We have a long walk ahead of us," I smirk.

"What does he mean by that?" Gage looks at Damon. "What does he mean?"

I am aware of Damon's sigh. "These tunnels move through the entire city. If we go the right way, we should get home undetected."

A loud crash rumbles the tunnels. "keep moving," I instruct.

"What was that?" Miles asks.

"Well, that was the house we just escaped from being blown into a million pieces. Bet you are glad for this rat-infested tunnel now, aren't you?" He just nods as he jogs to keep up with Damon and Gage, who are walking at a fast pace to get out of this dank place.

It was dark down here and the only light that paved the way were the flashlights on our phones. As we trudged through the dark tunnels, our senses were filled with the echoes of our footsteps, the squelching of water beneath our shoes, and the rats' squeals as they hurriedly fled from us.

It felt like we had been walking for hours and the damp stench had made its way around us. The stench would in grain itself into my soul. I would be smelling the damp, musky smell for days. I'd never get it out of my clothes. It annoyed me I had to move on the day I was supposed to start my new job. A smirk fell across my lips. Ava's bodyguard. It was almost—too easy.

"I'm glad you find this amusing. Any other grand adventures you want to take us on, Chase?" I look in front of me to see Damon glaring daggers into my soul.

"Oh, come on, did I ruin your busy schedule?"

"You put a target on all our backs and I still don't know why," He screams at me.

"Rossi was trafficking children—children, you would have done the same." I sigh.

Footsteps approach me and I feel Gage slap me on the back. "Wow, so you have some humanity—you never cease to amaze me."

"Fuck you, keep moving if you want to get there before light." He sneers at me while turning his back and walking the way he had come. I wasn't heartless. I could kill a man and feel nothing but not a child. They were innocent. Why would you want to harm something defenceless? That would be like harming an injured bird.

"Chase," I look up to see my brother waiting for me and a groan leaves my throat because I'm just awaiting the lecture that I know will follow once he opens his mouth. "This thing with Ava." He moves his hand through his hair. "It needs to stop." Ah, there it was, the start of a lecture I didn't want to hear.

"Why are you so interested in the well-being of the little beast?"

"Fuck, you've given her a nickname?" He stares at me. "What is wrong with you?"

"Like today or in general," I smirk.

"You're not going to stop, are you?"

"Why? When I'm having so much fun taunting the little beast."

"This is going to end badly."

"Yeah, yeah, that's what you always say. Come on, we can't allow those two to win the race home."

* * *

By the time we had come to the end of our destination, we were all muddy and black from our underground walk. Damon had done nothing but complain the entire way, and after a while, I had learned to just turn it off. Block him out like a white static noise. The peace was blissful. Sure he spoke, but I didn't catch a single word he was saying.

I made my way up the steel steps that led to our gardens. A sense of relief washed over me once the frosty night air filled my lungs. It's strange the things we take for granted. Now that

I'm in the open air, I can breathe freely, unlike in the confined space where my breathing was restricted.

"How long until he comes here?" Damon scowls as I enter through the main door. I have walked into the estate and he's already breathing down my neck.

"Have a day off." I grit.

"A day off? We've just been hunted and you want me to have a day off?" He screams like I'm not standing right next to him.

"I already told you, I will sort it." I rub my temples to let the tension of Damon drip from my body.

"When? When are you going to sort it, Chase? And what are we supposed to do in the meantime while you play house with your plaything?"

"I have a plan."

"Oh, well, that changes things." A wide smile appears on his face, and I watch as he turns to Gage and Miles. "He has a plan. A plan. Wonderful." He claps his hands together and his head snaps back towards mine. "I would love to hear your fucking plan."

"Not now." I grit out.

"Oh, so you don't have a plan." He smirks. "Of course you don't, just going to wing it, are you, brother?"

"I'm dirty and I'm tired. I don't need this shit."

"Oh, by all means, go freshen up, Princess." I shake my head as I walk away from him because there was no talking to him when he was like this. I knew I fucked up. I didn't need him to remind me.

As I step into my private bathroom, I begin to disrobe the wet and dirty clothes from my body, feeling a sense of contentment as I sense the water jets from the shower cascade across my body. The day had taken a strange turn, but I knew it was coming. I just didn't expect Nikoli to wait so long to come find me.

Guilt consumed me for involving Damon, Gage, and Miles in my nonsense. It wasn't their fight, but it had thrown them into the shit like with me, and why? Because I had lost focus, I had been so obsessed with teaching the little beast a lesson I had forgotten there was a bigger threat in the midst.

That was my fuck up.

I didn't regret taking out Rossi and, given the chance, I would do it all again. I could still relive the memory of his burning flesh. It gave me great pleasure anytime my mind wandered back to that night. He got what he deserved. That wasn't my fuck up. My fuck up was not going after Nikoli and his band of merry men before he came after me.

I wished I could just forget about the little beast, leave her to the mundane insignificant life she had set up, but I couldn't. I had seen her, tasted her, smelt her, and I wanted more. The water cascades down my body, but my mind can just see her perfect little body, how she wriggled when I touched her, the slight little moans that fell from her lips. I look down and I'm hard as a fucking rock.

Fuck, why did she affect me like this?

I run my fingers through my hair, sighing, my cock throbs and my hands slide down my body. With my eyes closed, I can see her in here with me. I press her perfect little body against the wall. My hands grip hold of my throbbing cock. It's slick and wet as I glide my hands up and down my cock.

I can see her, every—fucking—part; of; her. Her sweet little voice sings to me, "Do it, Chase, do it for me, cum for me."

My breathing grows heavy as I jerk my cock faster, envisioning her on her knees in front of me, those cock sucking lips open and ready for me to slide past her lips and enter the depths of her hot, wet mouth.

"Cum for me," I hear her sweet voice as I envision my cock wrapped around her lips, pushing further inside of her, the way her tongue should massage me into fucking oblivion. My hand moves faster with the image of her sucking me harder and faster, begging me to cum for her.

My head flies back as I experience the pangs of desire tightly seize me. Relentlessly pushing closer and closer to the edge. The desire crawls through me at an alarming rate. One more tight tug and I groan out my release and allow my desire to wash down the drain with the dirt and grime of the day.

I pant, my palms hitting the stone tiles as I steady myself against the shower and feel the warm water cascading down my body as I try to steady my breath from the fantasy that is my enemy. Bowing my head, I released a sigh of frustration.

Little beast, what are you doing to me?

6

BODYGUARD FOR HIRE

AVA

I don't know how many times I have paced up and down waiting for the elusive bodyguard that I had agreed to meet but it was that or cower at home and hope the mysterious stalker didn't enter my home and do whatever vile things he had planned for me.

"You're going to wear a hole in the floor." She gasps.

"Well, promptness is not his forte. Maybe this is a bad idea."

"Ava, he ha

"Ava, he has dropped everything to travel to the middle of nowhere to come and see you. While his timekeeping skills are questionable, he's your best option tonight. So, please, sit down. You're making me dizzy."

I'm about to walk towards her because, of course, she is right. He is doing me a favour here and what am I doing? Grumbling about the length of time it's taking him to arrive. I give my head a shake and hope it jolts some sense into me when I notice a loud knock and start bouncing up and down while screaming like a little girl.

"Jesus, Ava, will you calm down? That's him."

"Are you sure?" I whisper.

"No, the psycho knocked on the door today." She rolls her eyes as she walks away from me. To greet the man who I was hoping would be the answer to all my problems.

I can pick up on their indistinct words, but I cannot comprehend their message. It must be good though, because I can detect Audrey's laughter before she enters the room. With my body positioned and my hands on my hips, I patiently wait for the elusive bodyguard to arrive with her, but there is nothing.

"Well?" I ask her, getting more annoyed at this entire situation.

"This is Chase." She sneers as she steps aside and I meet the very late bodyguard who will save me from my doom. A crease forms at my brow, well you don't see that every day.

"You are the bodyguard?" I ask, peering at him and trying to figure out why he looks like that. God! I can't take him seriously. How was a psycho stalker supposed to take him seriously, although he carried an air of intimidation—so it could work—perhaps?

Oh, who was I kidding? He looked fucking ridiculous.

"Is it a prank you're both playing? if it is, then I can tell you right now, I'm not in the mood." It had to be a prank. What other explanation was there for this—ridiculousness?

"A prank?" I hear his deep voice. "Now why the fuck would I drive to the middle of nowhere to prank miss prim and fucking proper? Not only was his appearance laughable, but he also had a negative attitude. Perfect.

My eyes glide across his frame as I assess the man in front of me who is supposed to protect me. Tall muscles bulging everywhere! Dressed all in black, I think I can faintly see the swirling hues of his crystalline blue eyes, but he has no face. How am I supposed to trust somebody I can't see? No, instead of a glimpse of his face, I am greeted with a skeleton mask. I roll my eyes. I mean, was that necessary?

"I'm no expert, of course, but is it Halloween?"

A small chuckle bubbles from his throat. "Not that I'm aware of. Why do you ask?"

"The mask. What's with the mask?"

"In this line of work, I prefer to keep my identity hidden until I can trust you."

"Oh, and you don't trust me?"

"Well, I don't know you, Miss Valentina. Do you trust me?" I shake my head. "Well, there you go. I think we will get on just fine."

"Audrey, a word." I watch her roll her eyes as she saunters into the kitchen with me. Gazing at the curve of the kitchen, he remains stationary. Swiftly turning my head back to Audrey,

I give her a penetrating stare. "Okay, Audrey, what the hell?"

"Yeah, I'm not sure what's going on. He's not so shy about his appearance, but it gives him an edge, don't you think?" She smiled.

"Yeah, sure, an edge of psycho."

"He not that bad, Ava. When I say he's the best at what he does, I mean it. So, what if he's a little quirky and theatrical? Your safety is all that matters. If he can keep you safe, let him hide behind his mask."

I walk back towards the creepy skeleton man intent on doing just as Audrey had said because feeling safe was the only thing I wanted but it was strange as I stood before him, I just couldn't do it.

"Are you going to take off the mask?"

"No." He answers.

"Then, I guess we are done here." He takes a step towards me and my heart races. He smells dangerous and musky, like crisp spice on an autumn day that makes you feel at peace and nostalgic. "What are you doing?" I ask, to which I'm once again ignored. He takes another step towards me until he's invading my space. "Okay." I hold a hand up. "That's close enough buddy,"

"Buddy," he repeats with a hint of amusement in his mysterious tone.

"Have you not heard of personal space?"

He keeps moving forward until I can feel the heat from his muscular body press up against mine. "I have, but I enjoy invading it." He whispers in my ear and fuck! That whisper sends butterflies crawling through my body.

My head is spinning, and I'm not even sure why. "If you—won't take the mask off, then I think we are done here." I stutter out.

"Well," his fingers slide across my face and as they tease my skin, a slow moan falls from the back of my throat. He takes a step back, but I doubt he is as surprised as I am. I just look at him wide-eyed. "In case you change your mind." He places a card in my hand, turns and walks away from me.

I just stand there staring at the space in which he inhabited. Even with the mask on, he had left an impression. Yes, it was best that he left. Nothing good would come of having that man around. Nothing good at all.

"So, are we well acquainted?" Audrey comes running towards me. "Where is Chase?" She accuses. I shake my head, "Ava?"

"He wouldn't take the mask off."

"Okay?"

"So, I told him to leave," I mutter.

"You did what?" She screams, busting my eardrum. "Do you know how hard it is to get him to work with you? Especially on a job like this."

"A job like this?"

"He prefers tracking people. I can't believe you'd do this, Ava. He came a long way just to help you and—."

"Well, he wouldn't take the mask off." I repeat. She shakes her head at me. "We don't need him, anyway." I sigh.

"Oh?" She gives me that sly smirk. "What about your stalker?"

"Well—." I'm stumped. She was right. What about my stalker? I had just sent away the only person who didn't question my sanity with the shadowy figure who wouldn't leave me alone. And why? Because he had worn a mask. Stupid, stupid Ava.

"Ava, I can call him—." She looks at me with pity, and that's a look I don't want to see. After all the experiences I had encountered in my life, I had never received that expression from Audrey, and I wasn't beginning to receive it now.

"No," I hold my hands up. "I will not let some creep rule my life. I also don't need a creepy dude in a mask watching me."

"Ava—."

"What time are we going out?" I ask her because I've had enough of her pitiful looks.

"You still want to go out?" Her mouth gapes open and she looks at me like I'm the one who's lost the plot.

"Why wouldn't I," I smirk. Once again, I'm pitied. "We are going. We are going to have a damn good time, so stop looking at me like I'm made of glass and could break at any moment."

"Okay, we will go out." She smiles like I've convinced her.

Upon entering **THE BOOK CLUB**, the atmosphere appeared spacious. This was my favourite hangout spot to wind down. There was no chance of bumping into anyone you knew at the book club, making it a secluded spot. It was a hidden gem. Where else could you chat, dance, and read books on a night out? It was my favourite place in New York. I only came here when I came to the city.

The dim lighting set a romantic and ambient atmosphere. The bars were stretched out into the far corners, winding around the room, but it was what was upstairs when you walked up the midnight winding staircase that was the true treasure. Rows upon rows of books filled this little hideaway in oak bookshelves with little twinkling lights leading the way.

Step by step, I make my way up the winding staircase, finally finding relaxation. Everyone should have a place where they have a sense of security. It used to be my home, but now, that is not my safety net. That place became the breeding ground for nightmares. I wondered who I had pissed off to warrant such an invasion of privacy. I must display the annoyance on my face as I reach the hidden book nook.

"It's not that bad." The stranger smiles. Studying the enigmatic man, he positions himself in one of the leather-bound chairs, with one leg crossed over the other and a book grasped in his hand.

"Excuse me?"

"You don't look happy. It can't be that bad. Books take you to another world." He smiles.

"Yes, yes, they do." I smile back, walking towards the bookshelf and skimming my fingers across the vast amount of books before carefully pulling out my secret vice—a romance because that's what my life severely lacked.

I often enjoyed reading about the story unfolding, and how we perceived love to be because on the surface I had never experienced love—or something similar. So, I liked to escape from time to time and get lost in the fantasy that one day love would come, even though I knew that couldn't happen.

I didn't even notice he had edged closer until I heard the shuffling of the seat beside me. Perhaps if I disregarded him, he would leave, but I sensed his gaze fixated on me, his intense stare piercing through my already anxious body.

"Romance?" He quizzes me. "Now, why would someone like you need to read about romance?"

"Someone like me?" I finally gasped, taking my nose from my book and doing what Audrey said I should do more and socialise.

"Well—." He pushes his finger across his chin and I finally take him in. He's not bad-looking, with dark hair, big chestnut eyes and a smile that could melt the ice caps. "I wouldn't think you would be short on romance." He winks.

"Are you flirting with me?" I smirk.

"I was trying to—evidently, I seem to have failed."

A small smile appears on my lips. "You are doing just fine. I guess I'm just not used to it."

"How is that possible?"

It could be the case that you shouldn't judge a book by its

cover.

"Maybe I shouldn't, but people still do." He smiles. "I can leave you to your book if you like. I'm Mike, by the way." He holds his hand out, and that's when I realise that I'm not going to get the peace I was searching for, not here, not with him anyway.

"It's nice to meet you, Mike," I take his hand in mine and the warmth of his touch makes me smile. "I'm Ava."

"Such a pretty name for a pretty girl." And I'm blushing. Me? I'm fucking blushing. Could I be any more transparent?

"You don't get compliments often either?" I shake my head, "well, that's just a crime, pink suits you." He smirks while looking at my now-flushed face. "Would you like to go out with me if you aren't opposed to some real romance?" he asks.

"Oh," my face must be showing the shock that I'm positive is clear.

"If you like, that is." A crease of confusion forms across his brow. His hand still holds mine and I feel his thumb move in circles across my fingers and it is oddly soothing that I let out a contented sigh.

"I leave you for two minutes and you've already pulled." Audrey shrieks and Mike quickly releases my hand, but doesn't drop eye contact.

"Busted," he whispers, so only I can hear, and a chuckle flies out of my mouth.

"Audrey, I thought you went to go make the drinks. You were gone that long." She rolls her eyes and I look at her empty hands. "And you still have no drinks," I smirk.

"Oh shoot, must have forgotten them." She smiles, "I actually came to find you because I need to go home, so are you ready?"

We had just arrived. What was she talking about? Was I ready? On any other night, I would jump at the chance to race home because often I didn't want to be out anyway, but right now, it was strange. I didn't want to leave.

"You know, I think I might stay for a while."

"Really?"

"Yeah, I'm enjoying myself and a few drinks before I leave will do me good, I think." I'm not sure if I'm trying to convince her or myself.

"I can't leave you here all alone."

"I'm not alone." I nod my head towards the man who had invaded my peace. "I'm sure Mike can entertain me."

"Oh, I'm sure he can." She smirks. "You let me know when you're on your way home, so I know you got home safe." She commands.

"Of course." I smile while letting her wrap me in a warm hug as she plants a kiss on my cheek.

"Oh, and you, look after my girl—," Mike gives her an amused smile. "Or they'll never find your body." She warns.

I watch her walk back down the stairs and shake my head. As I turn my eyes towards Mike, he genuinely looks terrified, and rightfully so. Audrey never made an empty threat and as cute as she looked, she never made a threat she hadn't followed through with.

"She's a little—intense." He finally breaks the silence.

"She's just protective." I laugh. "She means well."

The night is more relaxed once Mike has gotten over the initial shock of being threatened by a woman that he probably thought he could squish. She may be small, but she was mighty.

The drinks flowed freely, and I was completely relaxed. Mike was an interesting man. Not only did he love to read books, but he also owned a library in the city. I was swooning right there and then. It was like he had fallen out of a romance novel—and I was getting ahead of myself.

Venturing out into the dark night air, the wind bites at my cheeks and he stands at the side of the curb, whistling and calling the cab. "Now, your friend can leave my body intact." He winks.

"She sure can. Would you like a lift?" I politely ask.

"Not today, but your number would be nice—unless that's crossing a line." God, he was so polite and perfect. Did he have any flaws? I hand him my phone and watch as he punches in his number and when he passes me his phone, I do the same.

"Maybe we will both get the romance we have been missing." He whispers in my ear as his enormous arms wrap around my body, cocooning me in his sweet warmth. God, he felt so perfect.

I feel his lips brush against my cheek and it has been that long since a man has touched me that shivers pulse through my body and a contented sigh passes my lips. "Goodnight, beautiful, Ava."

"Goodnight, Mike." I smile as I enter the cab and watch him watching me on the sidewalk as the cab pulls away from view.

Laying back, I smile, not a forced smile for my fans. Not a forced smile for Audrey so that she won't worry, but an actual genuine smile that reaches to my eyes because it may turn into nothing. Though it may not be a happily ever after scenario, I'm grateful for what it is now. I appreciate the warmth.

As I step out of the cab, I am filled with a sense of calmness. Life is good. I had an enjoyable night for once. I wasn't on edge and my little stalker friend had all but disappeared.

There's a chance that I would have a peaceful night's sleep in the end.

The smile on my face fades as I reach my front door, and I notice a piece of paper pinned to it with a Swiss Army knife. A groan falls from my lips as I peer at the words scribbled on the pasty white piece of paper that flaps in the wind.

Little beast.

Playing with things you shouldn't.

Don't worry,

I know how much you love reading romance,

So, I gave you a heart to save HIM from breaking yours.

You're welcome.

GHOST.

Fuck. This guy was fucking crazy. I look around, but I can't see anything. There is complete silence, except for the intense pulsation of my heart. Looking down, there is a small black box. Oh, of course, the heart he threatened he left. I roll my eyes as I lean down and pick up that box.

I stare at that bloody box like it appeared from out of space.

There couldn't be a heart in there, right? He wouldn't kill someone I had chatted to just to prove a point, would he? Oh shit. That's when I realised he was there. The entire damn time that I experienced freedom, he was there—watching me.

As I lift the lid, I glance inside and a wave of shock washes over me. This guy was fucking nuts. There was a heart sitting in that box, but that wasn't the worst part. Underneath the heart was the book I had been reading. A scream emits from my throat as I drop the box to the ground. Not only had he sacrificed a nice man, but he had ruined a good fucking book with his blood.

I was unsure if I was in a state of shock, as I grew more irritated by the fact that he had spoiled the book, and then tears started to fall from my eyes. A night that had given me hope had turned into one that would give me nightmares and I was here—all alone. I had told Audrey I was in the cab, so nobody could help me.

What if he was just in there—waiting?

The tremors of fear crawled around my body like snakes wiggling around beneath my skin. I was standing motionless with fear, rooted to the spot. Scared to enter my house because of the fear that he lurked within waiting to pounce.

I swung open the door, but it met me with silence. I shake my head at my stupidity, well what did I expect he would jump out and announce himself? Why would he? He hadn't announced his presence so far, just hinted that he was around.

As I enter the house, I longed to escape. A sigh escapes my throat while I stroll into the home that was once my sanctuary. My eyes scan the area, and nothing is out of place. It looks as I had left it.

I take slow steps, sauntering into the kitchen. I'm on edge, looking around to make sure I'm alone and I am. There on the counter sits a filled champagne flute with a pink Post-it note attached: thought you could use a little wind-down time, Audrey xx.

My eyes peer at the note untrusting. The bubbles rise to the surface. Well, if Audrey sent it, why not? I pick up the glass and walk straight upstairs to my bedroom. I placed the glass on my nightstand. Maybe it would help me sleep. getting changed, I pick the glass up and empty the entire contents down my throat. "Thanks, Audrey," I mutter out loud.

I stumble near the bed, holding onto the bed to steady my fall.

A dizzying emotion gallops through my body. I can see. My vision distorts everything. A mist covers my vision and the only thing I can see are shapes. Fuck. What was in that drink? My head is filled with hazy thoughts, and my body is weak, but I can't sit down for fear of losing consciousness.

That's when I see it. The shape of a figure enters my room. I try to blink my eyes, but my vision doesn't change. Hunched over onto the bed, I crawl onto it because I have nowhere else to go. The sound of heavy footsteps grows closer and closer, then my head hits the pillow.

"Do you remember me yet?" I detect a voice in my ear. I shake my head. What was I supposed to be remembering? "Oh, little beast, you will remember—I will make you remember." The voice threatens.

His body smothers mine. I am aware of his breath brushing against my skin. The mist that had covered my eyes is still present, and everything is just wavy shapes. The man's ultrasonic voice leaves no space in my mind as he invades my personal bubble. As he lingers nearby, his breath against my skin becomes increasingly erratic, sending tingles through me.

As he pulls down the straps on my negligee, I want to voice my objection. I want to move, but I am immobile. I can't scream. The only screams I hear are inside of my head. I want to scream what am I supposed to be remembering, but the only noise that comes out is a tiny squeak.

"This must be so hard." Overwhelmed with a sense of vulnerability reminiscent of a small girl. "How does it feel to be tricked, little beast?" A squeak falls from my lips because I don't have a clue what he's fucking talking about.

His hands run down my body. Every light touch sends tingles running through my body. He's barely touched me and my body is shaking. I sense the silk material slipping away from my body. "Like a pretty little doll that I can use for my enjoyment." He whispers once more. "Do you remember yet?" I shake my head. He seems annoyed by my response.

His hands grip my waist with force and I want to cry out, but no sound comes out. The overwhelming sensation intensifies and I can hear his indistinct words, but I can no longer comprehend what he says. My eyes threatened to close and darkness consumed my body as my body relaxed and I sank into the abyss that I could feel pulling me under.

7

YOU ARE MINE

CHASE

She remains motionless. Her serene appearance masks her continued consciousness, clear through her deep breathing. She should have remembered. Why didn't she fucking remember? She sucked me dry of all my assets. Was I that insignificant that she would forget?

I would not touch her like this. I just wanted to humiliate her and make her seem insignificant and defenseless. Just as she impacted me earlier. The rage ripped through my soul. It was strange, though. Observing her in such a vulnerable state stirred up emotions within me. It was a mistake moving closer to her because once my body touched hers—I felt — well; I felt alive again.

Nothing comes from her lips as she parts those delectable plump lips but small little squeaks and if that cute little noise alone doesn't make my cock almost jump out of my pants. Fuck. Why does she have this effect on me?

It was a mistake moving against her like this. No, it was a mistake removing her clothes from her body. Throughout that process, she emitted squeaks. She knew that I exposed her to me despite that. She wouldn't speak.

I yearned to catch her voice as much as I needed air to respire. I knew she hadn't lost her lost her speech. The drug may render her immobile and her vision distorted, but her speech was intact. We had tried these months ago because I wanted to listen to her, but once again she had left me disappointed.

My hands run down her body, gripping her inner thighs as I rip her legs apart. She remembered that part. Her eyes are closed, but once I slide her legs open, little moans fall from her lips. Oh, maybe she remembered. Isn't that what had excited her so much all those years ago?

"Now, little beast, you don't remember me." My fingers slide down her inner thighs. "But you remember this," I smirk while dipping my head between the crevice of her thighs and running my nose along her already wet slit. Fuck, she smells as sweet as she did all those years ago.

My tongue glides across her pussy, and I sense the motion from her body beneath my touch. Ah, the little beast, must be waking up. My tongue comes down against her pussy, but this time it won't be slow because I'm fucking starving.

Curving my tongue, I enter her, and the loud moans are music to my fucking ears. Imprinting my fingers into her flesh and burying my face deeper into her slick center, every stroke of my tongue leaves her enticing flavor and the resounding bursts of her moans have me throbbing with passion.

"Oh god, oh god." I hear her cry out. My lips come down across her lips and her pussy muffles my own moans as my tongue pushes harder and faster deep within her core.

Absorbing every drop of her essence, I sense her body quake beneath me, her legs convulsing as she lets out a scream and empties all of her intoxicating juices into my mouth, swallowing every bit that my tongue expels from her and gliding over her lips, capturing any evidence of her desire.

The silence falls around us. All I can hear is her deep breaths of sleep as her chest rises and falls. I maneuver around her body like a ninja replacing the clothes that I should have never taken off.

The moonlight shines through her open window and I can't help thinking how ethereal she looks in this light.

How could something so sinister be so beautiful?

Positioned by the window, I released a sigh. She had captivated me then, just like she was doing right now. I reach my hand into my pocket, retrieve the pad, and unfold it to reveal a blank sheet of paper.

Seated near the window, being mindful to not obstruct the moon's glow, I retrieve my charcoal crayon and start the process of drawing the little beast that haunted my mind.

I drew every form of her perfect features, except her beautiful, captivating eyes. I drew her just as I saw her. I wanted her to know I was here, watching her while she slept.

Inspecting the portrait I've drawn of her. A smile emerges

on my face. Even on paper, she looks perfect. Finishing it by appending a concise two-word signature. Little beast.

removing the page from the pad and walking to her night-stand, I place it with a single red rose sitting on top.

She would be my undoing, but I couldn't stay away—even if I wanted to.

I walk away into the night thinking about the girl that stole more than my money. I had doubts about how much revenge I wanted to pursue, but I was conscious of the fact that the longer I lingered near her, the more enticed I became by her trap.

my intention was for her to comprehend the emotions I had experienced upon discovering she had taken advantage of me, but whenever I was near her—I longed for something beyond that.

I just wasn't sure what more I could want from her—she wouldn't give me it even if I knew.

So, for now, this was enough.

She didn't know it yet, but she was mine.

Ava had taken from me and now she would give me back what she had taken, one way or another—she would give herself to me.

Little girls shouldn't play games they can't possibly win.

I stay, I watch her from the woods as she gets up. Poor little thing looks confused, probably thinks she dreamed me up.

Then she walks towards the nightstand and I smile, awaiting the fear that I know will hit her body in mere moments.

She picks up the rose and a grimace crosses her face and this is it, the moment I have been waiting for. Her eyes fall on the sheet of paper I left for her to find, picking it up, I watch as she studies it.

It feels like a lifetime has passed and then the little beast does something I don't expect—she holds that piece of paper to her chest and she smiles. She fucking smiles.

Where was the fear?

Where was the terror that I had been there while she slept?

Where was the torture?

It seemed that on this day, I was the only one that was tortured and the little beast had found peace.

Uncertainty crawls through my body at an alarming rate and something rather unwelcome. Watching her smile at the torturous gift I had left spreads warmth through my body.

"God dammit, little beast, why couldn't you just fear me." I grit into the cold morning air.

I'm not going to fall for it again. I'm not going to fall for her again. So, why can't I peel my eyes from the little vixen?

I shake my head as I finally walk away from her but I can't help the feeling of loss every time I do this.

Watching Ava was supposed to haunt her but it seemed that the only one haunted here was....me.

8

I wake up alone. The negligee is still wrapped around my body. Did I dream it up? Was I that hungry for affection that I dreamt my stalker snuck into my room in the middle of the night to please me? A groan falls from my lips. Great, I'm losing the plot. He had done it, drove me to insanity.

A pounding erupts through the house. Or maybe that was inside my head, too. My head is overcome with a floating and painful sensation, as if I've just been in a boxing match with Mike Tyson. I had drunk a little but felt like I was suffering the after-effects of a wild night on the town.

Once more the pounding erupted, but then I realised it wasn't coming from inside of my head. Climbing out of bed, I race down the stairs. It was Audrey. She always had impeccable timing, and she wanted to find out what happened with the dashing bookkeeper who had held my attention enough for me to want to stay out.

Oh shit. Then I remembered the heart in the box. Shit. The fear stops my body at the foot of the stairs. I didn't know what was real and what wasn't real anymore. I wasn't sure what was real anymore. I wasn't sure if I dreamed it all up in my head or if it happened. Please let it be the warped confines of my deluded brain, I beg.

With the door swinging open, my mouth hung open, and I had the urge to close it once more. Oh no, what was he doing here? He just stands there with his deep penetrative gaze burning a hole through my soul. The skeleton mask still covers his face. "Why are you back?" I utter.

"You called me."

"When? I've only just woke up." I know that I'm standing before him wearing next to nothing and I still haven't moved.

This is worse than the walk of shame, which I would prefer. At least there was pleasure involved there. There was nothing pleasurable about this meeting.

"Are you going to invite me in?" What was he, a bloody vampire? Did he need an invitation to step across the threshold? A small chuckle falls from my lips. "I'm glad I amuse you, Miss Valentina."

"You don't." I scowl while stepping aside and allowing him to walk into my house—where I was alone. Smart, Ava. Very smart.

"I will wait here." He announced as I closed the door. "I said I will wait here."

"I heard you. I'm not deaf." He stands there, not moving. "What are you waiting for?"

"Well, I thought you might be more comfortable with clothes on." His eyes move up and down my body. "However, I'm not opposed to you staying as you are."

"I bet," I smirk. "You don't have to stand like a statue. Make yourself useful and make some coffee." I don't wait for a response as I leave him to mutter to himself.

I'm not one to put much thought into what I wear because the only people who would ever see it are myself, Audrey, and the fanbase I had gained over the years. I didn't care what the skeleton man thought of me. I had never seen his face. Why would I care what he thought? And yet here I am, staring into my closet like I don't have rows upon rows of clothes to choose from.

I make my way to the kitchen and he's sitting at the breakfast bar holding out a cup of coffee like he belongs here—in my house. "Thanks," I mutter, taking the cup from him.

"You sounded stressed when you called last night." He pauses and I'm still confused when I had the time to even call him. "Something about a heart in a box."

"Right, yes." I almost choked on my coffee at the mention of the heart that had been left as a gift. "I have to be honest. I don't remember calling you."

"Well, you were in a state, anyway I'm here to once again offer my services if you aren't opposed to how I appear." How he appeared? Oh right, the ridiculous mask. I shake my head. "Perfect, well, I accept your offer."

Did I offer him anything? Oh, I didn't have the energy to

argue with him, not today. Nothing made sense, and he was just confusing me even more. "You can accompany me to the firing range today, then." I smile.

He stands towering above me. "What do you need to go there for?"

"I need to learn how to protect myself, or wasn't that obvious?"

I feel his body push against mine and oh Holy fuck, did he feel good? I experience his warmth pressing against my back and his breath, revealing a secret to my skin as tingles of excitement travel down my spine. "What do you need to protect yourself for—" His head moves closer and I feel his warm breath hit my ear. "When you have me." He whispers in my ear.

"Oh, am I interrupting?" Audrey stands gasping in the doorway.

"Oh, Jesus Christ." I jumped up away from the bodyguard, who did not know about personal space. "Do you not know how to knock?" I accuse.

"Why" I accuse.

"Why would I need to knock when you leave the doors open?" She smirks. "I want to hear everything that happened between you and that gorgeous book geek."

"He wasn't a geek." I groan.

"You had a date?" He interrupts. "Does that happen often?" My head whips around and I glare at him, hoping that he will realise his mistake, but he just straightens his back and folds his arms across his chest, allowing the ripples of muscles to pop beneath his black shirt.

"Well, come on girl, I want details," Audrey squeals excitedly.

"I was speaking." He interrupts once more.

"I ignored you because it's none of your goddamn business."

"None of my business?" He takes a step towards me and my body shudders in response.

"That's right, it's none of your business. Why do you want to know, anyway?"

He takes another step towards me. He's close now. So close. His dark musky scent moves around my body like I'm basking in his dark and seductive, manly scent. "I like to know how many people I have to kill." He growls.

Audrey races between us both, pushing him back. I'm not sure how because he was six feet of pure muscle. Her hand rests on his chest as she nuzzles him away from my body. "Chase, best not scare her off. I'm curious. How did you find yourself back here?" Her head whips back towards me. "I thought creepy mask guy was fired?" She cocks a brow.

"I'm so glad that is catching on." He mutters.

"Well, you're the one who refuses to show your face." She rolls her eyes.

"I have my reasons. Now, how many dates are you going on?"

"None. I don't make a habit of meeting many men."

"That I doubt, sweetheart." A chuckle falls from his lips.

"What's that supposed to fucking mean? You don't even know me."

"I know enough."

"You know what?" He looks back at me. "I don't need this. You are strange, but that I can bypass. What I can't bypass is how fucking rude you are."

"Oh, I'm sorry, Princess, but I'm not here to massage your ego. I'm here to safeguard you, and must be informed about the people you spend time with."

"You're fucking unbelievable."

"Thanks,"

"That wasn't a compliment." I sigh. "You know what, just leave."

"If that's what you want." I nod. "Okay sweetheart, your funeral." He turns and walks away from me without another word.

"Can you believe that guy?" I gasp. Audrey shakes her head at me. "What? He started it."

"See, I am unsure of what has entered your mind, but you believed you had a need for him, otherwise why would he be present and because you are displeased with his attitude, you have once again sent him away?"

"Yeah, so."

"Swallow your pride and—" She points in the direction he walked in. "Go on, he's the only one who can help you." I scowl at her and let out an annoyed groan.

As I dash out of the kitchen, I notice him on the verge of walking out the door and leaving my life again. I took in a deep breath and hated that I needed him as much as I did. "Chase," I scream. I watch as he turns around. "I need you—please don't leave." I grit.

"Fine, but I'm not taking you to the firing range."

"Fine." I gasp.

As I turn away from him and breathe a sigh of relief. I'm kicking myself because he had won. He knew I needed him and I had to put up with his stupid mask, his arrogant attitude and his over growing need to invade my personal space, but what choice did I have? It was him or the stalker and I knew which I would rather have, and it wasn't the psycho who sent hearts as a token of affection.

Well, if he thought I was going to make this easy for him—he had another thing coming. He would soon learn that I had hired him and I was in charge, not the other way round.

He needed a reality check, and I was aware of how to deliver it.

9

WATCHING AVA

CHASE

Watching Ava was perfect on paper, but the reality was much more mundane. When I thought of Ava, I thought of her back then. Back when I had met her. She was always partying, jumping from club to club and guy to guy, but this Ava, this Ava, was boring.

She did the usual mundane things. I had been watching her for three months and for three months Damon had breathed down my neck to just get it over and done with but I was a perfectionist and today wasn't the day to announce my identity but oh how I wish it was because if I had to sit in this house as she pottered about for one more day; I think I might blow my own brains out.

Making my way back to the house after ensuring the perimeter is safe—alone. It still made me chuckle that the thing she feared was living in her house with her. I had done some fucked up things over the years but this—this was just comical. She thought she was the master of deceit and she still hadn't figured out who was haunting her. Ava had gotten stupid over the years.

I walk through the house, but I'm met with silence. Well, this didn't seem right. Ava is nowhere to be seen, but she was here before I left, so where had my little beast gotten to? The panic hits my body as I walk into each room and find it empty. "Damn it, where is she?" I curse out loud.

Then I see her lying in a hammock in the library, a book resting on her chest, and a frown pierces my brow. Had she fallen asleep while reading? She looked so innocent, but I knew better. She wasn't innocent. That's how she tricked me the first time. I wasn't falling for it again. My feet move towards her, and out of curiosity, I lean down and pick up the book she had been reading before she fell into her peaceful slumber.

"Let's see what keeps your nose in a book," I mutter.

"Be mine," he growls once more.

Gently, he moves his fingers over my lips. The only sound in the room is the squelch of wetness and heavy breathing. I cry out as his fingers enter my wet opening and hold on to his shoulder.

The skilled touch of his fingers sends a thrilling surge through my body as I'm pressed against the wall. I'm uncertain of what he's cursing at until the sound of the zipper descending reaches my ears. Noticing my leg lifted high, I realize my body being pushed further into the wall. The slight twinge in my groin pinches at being stretched.

Shit. This was not literature—oh, Ava, you naughty girl. Fuck, she was reading—this before she fell asleep? I wonder how wet this makes her, a forbidden fantasy that only exists in her books and her head. This turns her on? My eyes pour over the words in her book and try as I might, I just can't tear my eyes away from the filth inked on the pages within.

Positioned in the cozy leather chair facing her, I sit down and pour over the words. My eyes widen more than once. I have never been much of a reader. What did I need to read for when my entire life had been more entertaining than what you would find along the pages of any book? I want to put the damn book down, but I'm enjoying the filth and drama that lay within the pages. Each time I read a scene between the couple, my cock throbs and I look over at the peaceful Ava wondering what she would think if we reenacted her filthy books scenes.

Is that what she wanted to be tied up and spanked like a naughty fucking girl while I pounded deep inside of that tight little pussy that had brought me to my fucking knees? Fuck, imagine a book causing this many emotions. I drop the book on the floor because if I keep reading the damn book, I'm going to be too far gone to stop myself from walking across this room and taking what I want.

I can sense the weight of my eyes increasing. Why was this chair so damn comfortable? Her scent is everywhere in this room, floral and sweet. It swarms around my head, giving me a sliver of nostalgia to the night that I could never forget.

I detect the movement of footsteps nearing me, but my eyes are shut. Not that she would know. The sweat drips down my neck. I needed a goddamn medal for surviving the heat from wearing this mask all the time. It was almost akin to the sensation I would envision as torture, but it maintained my hidden identity, so it justified the glistening perspiration trickling down my face.

Her body presses against mine and oh Holy fuck! She better move and she better move fast because I was in the mood to fucking devour her, but she doesn't move. Her small hand rests beneath the mask. Well, this was interesting. The little beast was getting brave.

My hand shoots out gripping hold of her small wrist, her body comes crashing down against mine. "What are you doing?" She gasps. My other hand grips her ass, pulling her further onto my knee. "You can let me go now." She whispers.

My hand crawls from her pert little ass to her delicate little neck. Pulling her head towards mine. "Is that what you want?" She nods. "Then tell me why you're grinding on my leg." Her movements don't stop, but her breathing is rasping. My hands move to her hips, gripping onto her, moving her body against my leg. "Come on, make a mess," I growl.

As I gaze at her face, she has taken on a beautiful rosy hue. She looks anywhere but at me, with her eyes facing down, "I–I can't." She stutters. My hands move her hips faster, and now she's panting. Fuck, if she gets any closer, she will feel how fucking hard I am for her. My hands move at a slower pace and I'm startled by the sensation of her warm, petite hands traveling across mine. "No," she utters, "Please—don't—stop." She pants.

Fuck, I wish she hadn't said that. I was hungry and the only thing that had stopped me from devouring her was her resistance, but now look at her, begging to make a mess all over me like a desperate little puppy. Fuck. I don't wait for her to protest, standing and allowing her to wrap her legs around my waist. A tiny squeal falls from her lips. "Where are you taking me?" A smirk falls across my lips. Not that she could see it. It amused me she would say the same thing she had said when I took her to my bed.

Walking to the bookshelves, I place her on the ground in front of the floor-length mirror. Shifting her body, I press her against the mirror and raise her small dress to her waist, leaving her only able to observe in the mirror as I retrieve my belt from my jeans. Moving her panties down those well-toned legs, my hands glide into the space between her thighs, pressing my nails into her skin. "Spread them," I growl, and just like before, she remains still.

My fingers press into her skin harder and I notice her yelp, but still she remains motionless. "Good girls, do as they are told," I whisper into her ear.

There is nothing but silence for a few moments. "Well, maybe I'm not a good girl." She gasps. Shit, she had that fucking right. My hands prize her legs apart until I can gain entry to her sweet pussy. My fingers glide up her thighs and shoot straight to her pussy. She throws her head back on my shoulder and lets out a slow moan. "Fuck, you're so fucking wet." I pant.

Moving my fingers away from her pussy, I insert my fingers down her throat. Waves of pleasure shoot down my spine when I hear her choking on my fingers as she consumes that delicious pussy juice down her throat.

Allowing my jeans to fall to the ground. I'm so fucking eager to enter her. She was right; she wasn't a good girl. "Bad girl," I gasp as I bend her body against the mirror, her gorgeous ass pushed out against my waiting cock. Fuck, I had waited months—for this.

Slipping my cock deep inside of her, she gasps and moans as soon as I enter her. Fuck, she feels just as tight as she did all those years ago. Pressing my body against hers, I enter her more deeply and sense her intense grip on me, as if I'm trapped in a vise. "Oh god, oh god, why does your dick feel so—fucking—good." She cries out.

Rotating my hips, I hit her with depth, causing both of us to gasp. Holding the belt, I struck her thighs. "Oh my god," she cries out. Fuck, the little beast liked it. My eyes widen with surprise and my cock jumps with excitement deep inside of her. Pressing her form against the mirror, I slide my cock up and down inside her at an escalating speed, alternating light strikes from my belt against her thighs. Her screams have my body shaking with desire.

Moving away from her and twirling her body around to face me I take my belt and grab both her arms up against the mirror tying her in a knot around the belt and looping it against the mirror so she can't escape, not that it looks like wants to escape right now. Excited gasps crawl out of her throat.

Gripping her ass in my hands, I dig my fingers into her flesh and hear her gasp. I half expect her to give me a look of fear, but I see nothing. Nothing but that glazed-over lustful look that I had come accustomed to seeing displayed across her pretty little face.

Lifting her, her legs envelop my waist and press my body against hers. "Tell me, Ava, is this the thing you read about—in those books?" I pant. Her eyes widen with surprise. "It's just a fantasy baby. Can I be yours?" I plead.

My cock enters her soaking wet pussy, and a loud moan falls from her lips. "Yes," she gasps, "Yes, you can—be my—fantasy." She moans her response. With each grip on her throat, I notice her pussy tightening around my cock as I push further inside of her. Her pussy is pulsing, begging me to release inside of her.

My cock is soaked from the desire that leaks from her tight, wet pussy. The desire pinches through me, causing me to move more forcefully within her. "Oh, fuck, why do you feel so fucking good?" I pant. The moans are screamed into my ear, but this only causes my cock to pump harder deep within her.

My grip on her throat tightens, and she gasps for fucking air, but I can't fucking stop—not even if I wanted to. I don't want to end her life. I should want to, but I don't. I yearn to continue being inside her soaking pussy, experiencing the overwhelming pleasure that runs through my body.

Pushing further until the pleasure courses through my body, I can hear her gasping for air, her glazed-over eyes showing me she's moments away from passing out. I can feel her pussy clench hard around my cock as she once again soaks my cock. "I should fucking hate you." I pant. "I should fucking hate you," I moan as I pour all of my desire into her dripping hole. "But I don't, goddamn you Ava, I don't," I whisper.

The grip on her throat loosens and wait for her to take the first breaths as the air enters her lungs. She sucks in the air that I had restricted and she looks at him. Confusion passes through her eyes. "You should hate me?" She gasps with wide eyes. "Why should you hate me?"

Shit, I wish I hadn't said that. I was getting too close. I should let her go and she would never know that the ghost from her past had found her. She would never know how close I had gotten to her and maybe she wouldn't hate me for what I'd done.

Is that why I couldn't show her who I was? Because I was

afraid she would see me and she would hate me? I shake my head. I don't care what she thinks. This wasn't about her feelings—this was about mine. However, the emotion of her despising me produces a sickening reaction in my body.

"Why would you hate me?" She asks again.

Lifting her small worn-out body and freeing her from the belt that had held her, her hands rest on my neck and she rests her head on my chest.

Oh, little beast, how I wish I could hate you. It would be easier that way.

Guiding her to her bed and settling her body into the silk sheets, I pick up on her murmur. "Why would you hate me?" She asks.

Positioned next to her, I run my fingers through her hair. Silky against my rough hands like a light has pierced a hold through my dark soul. That's what Ava was, she was light and me? I needed that light. My soul was hungry for it. "Don't ask questions you won't like the answer to," I murmur into her hair.

I moved away from her because it was getting dangerous to

be so close to her. If I wasn't careful, I wouldn't ever be able to let her go. I feel annoyed at myself because this wasn't supposed to happen. I wasn't supposed to fall for the beast; I was supposed to just get revenge, make her feel small and stupid, but maybe that wasn't the plan all along. Perhaps the plan all along was—this.

She grabs my hand before I can move too far away from her, pulling my body back against her. My eyebrows furrow in confusion as she wraps my arm around her body. Fuck. Too close. "Please don't leave me." She begs. "Please stay, at least until I fall asleep."

So, that's what I do. I stay there wrapped in her warm embrace. Noticing her warmth encompass an area I'd rather it didn't—to my heart. Her deep breathing tells me she's asleep, but still I don't move. I stay wrapped around her body like I've always belonged there.

I don't belong there. I know I don't belong there, but I want to be here. I want to be here with her just like this more than I've wanted anything. It's risky lying here. She could peel back the mask and see the face of her past. It's possible that I wished for her to remove it from my face, similar to ripping off a band-aid.

I would lose this feeling once she knew I would lose her, but for now, I wanted to stay here with the illusion that right now, in this moment, she was mine. And if I couldn't keep her forever, I would keep the illusion—just for now.

10

I WONDER

AVA

I wake up with the light streaming through the window and his arms are still wrapped around my body. I wake up feeling contented and safe. This is the first time in a long time I've felt safe.

I knew as soon as I had met him it was dangerous having this man so close, but the stalker had ceased to terrorize me since Chase had been here and I no longer had to live in fear.

The way he had touched my body and pushed the desire to course through my body, I could still feel the tremors that had coursed through my body, I had felt nothing like it before and when he had gripped my throat and I could breathe at first; I was afraid. Afraid that I would die, afraid that he could make me pass out and do whatever he wanted to my unconscious body, but the thing that surprised me more was that fear slipped away and all that was left was—nothing.

There were no thoughts. It was empty. All of my worries, everything that had plagued me it just fell away. It's like he knew how to reset my brain and he did it because he wanted to release me from the chains that had bound me to the prison. Something trapped me inside.

He could have left, but he was still there. I to turn in his arms to face him and I'm looking back at that bloody ridiculous mask. It was the strangest sex I had ever had, but didn't I want the fantasy? Yeah, it was all about the fantasy. Still, I was curious who was under there. Maybe he was hideous, and that's why he hid his face. I didn't believe his excuses of trust because what the hell was that? I didn't know faces amounted to trust, but maybe they did. Looking into someone's eyes can tell you more about a person than words ever could.

Maybe it was so exciting because it was like a fantasy. Me not knowing who hid behind the mask, but could I continue whatever the hell had happened here without seeing his face? I shake my head. I knew I couldn't do that. Every day with him, the temptation had grown, and I just had to know who he was, what he looked like. I had to know why he hid under that ridiculous mask. He had been here for months and he had never taken off that damn mask.

What if I didn't like what I saw once I revealed his face? Then what? Then would I be back to feeling unsafe and alone with my stalker? Speaking of my stalker, it was strange, the drawing he had left. Once I picked it up, I was sure I would feel fear knowing he had once again invaded my space and watched me while I slept, but I didn't. I was humbled by his gesture. I knew he was dangerous. The heart in the box had shown me what he was capable of, but I had a feeling he wouldn't hurt me. I'm not sure why, but once his gifts stopped, I'm ashamed to say that I miss them.

I shouldn't miss them. Hadn't I hoped and prayed that he would just go away and leave me alone? So why did I miss his presence? Maybe it was the fact that he was so infatuated with me he left a piece of himself behind. A token of the person he was underneath, all the stalking and skulking. There was a man who had displayed a weird way to show me he was here.

I had been alone so long that when he had appeared out of nowhere that the fear had clawed its way through my body and now he was gone, just like I had wanted, but I missed his presence. Sure, I felt safe, but when he was around as scared as I felt, it was the first time I ever felt alive. The adrenaline rush to get away from him had made me feel alive, and now I was back to nothing. Feeling nothing. Just existing.

I should be grateful, but I wasn't. I had had no one to care about me the way the shadow man had cared, and then Chase appeared and he disappeared. Was it the mask or the body-guard? I didn't know. All I knew was that I would never discover the identity of the man infatuated with me, but at least I would have little remnants that he left behind.

I sigh as I look at the skeleton mask I'm now facing. Well, moment of truth. I'm about to see the man behind the mask. My hand shakes as I move towards his face. Reaching my hand at the bottom of his mask once more, I pull the bottom of the mask and gasp as I feel his hand once more grip my wrist.

"You just can't help yourself, can you?"

I sigh in frustration. "Are you hideous under there?"

"Yes, Ava, my face is all mangled." He grits out.

"Really?" I ask with surprise.

"No, not really." He chuckled, "What is the obsession with seeing my face?"

"Well," my eyes dart around the round. "I'm just curious, I guess."

"Curious?"

"Yes, you've seen me. Why can't I see you?"

"I'm not ready yet."

"Chase, you fucked me yesterday and you still don't trust me?" I gasp.

He flips me onto my back, holding my wrists above my head. "No, Ava, I don't trust you. I never will." He utters.

"Never?" I gasp. "I have done nothing to cause you not to trust me."

"Ava, don't push me."

"Or what?" I scowl at him.

"Keep going and you'll find out."

"Just show me who you are," I scream. "How am I supposed to trust you when you won't even show me your fucking face?" The rage runs through my body at an alarming rate. "I let you into my home and you can't even show me your face. You fucking Coward." I spit at him.

He grabs my hands, pinning them together against the bed; he rummages in his trousers for something. I can hear the clank and I'm unsure of what the crazy bastard is doing now until I feel my hands being clicked into the handcuffs above my head. "What the fuck are you doing?" I scream.

"I warned you, if you kept on pushing, you'd find out."

"Find out what? That you're an even bigger psychopath than I gave you credit for."

"Oh baby, you keep talking dirty to me." He moves his head close to mine. "It turns me on." He presses his body hard against mine and I feel his hard cock press against my pelvis.

"Chase," I gasp.

"Oh, look at you, I've barely fucking touched you and you're already thinking about how good my cock would feel buried in that tight little pussy of yours."

I can feel the heat rise from my chest to my face at his dirty words. I'm lucky I can't see his face right now because I'm not sure I could look at him. The way his body presses against mine has the desire pulsing through my body and if he reached between my legs, he would find me dripping for him. I hadn't even seen his face, and he worked my body like he had learned it and memorized it.

He moves away from me, rummaging in a drawer. My eyebrows furrow in confusion. I'm at his mercy, with no way of getting away from him. The fantasy was exciting yesterday but I think I was over the fantasy now. This was moving way out of my comfort zone, and I wasn't sure I liked it.

He walks back towards me. "Look at you, so helpless, what's wrong? No smart words now." I shake my head. "Well, you still need to be punished for your smart mouth, and then you'll learn."

"Punished? Learn?" I gasp.

"Yes, Ava, what is it about those words that you don't understand?"

"Chase, this was fun, but you have to let me go now."

"I'm sorry, baby, but I don't have to do anything." He grips hold of my ankle, stretching my body as far as it can go down the bed. "You will learn." He grits out at me as he wraps the rope around my ankle, spreading both of my legs and pinning me to the bed.

"This is my punishment to lie in bed naked?" I raise a brow.

"Oh no, this is your punishment." My brows furrowed once more in confusion as I hear the buzzing from the vibrator that he twirls in his hand.

"You're going to punish me with an orgasm," I smirk.

He says nothing as he crawls between my legs. "Do you know how sweet you fucking smell? If you had been a good girl, I would have licked your delicious pussy until you came so fucking hard in my mouth." A squeak squeezes from my throat. "But you were a bad fucking girl," his fingers slide across my pussy. "And bad girls need to be punished. Fuck. You're fucking soaked already." He growls.

"Chase, please," I beg.

"Oh, it's a bit late for that now." He thrusts the vibrator deep inside of me and I swear my eyes roll into the back of my head. The vibrations hit me and the moans fall from my lips.

"There, not so bad, is it?" He mocks. While holding a smaller vibrator in his fingers, the light buzzing as he switches it on has my eyes widening.

"What are you doing with that?" I moan.

He straps the tiny vibrator to my clit and the intense desire crashes through my body. "Oh, fuck." I cry out. "Oh god, please, fuck." My body shakes with desire as I feel my body ride through my first orgasm.

He crawls up my body, making sure to not disturb the devices that are making me scream out my pleasure. "There you go, feeling good now, smart ass?"

"Yes, yes, yes," I scream. "Oh god, yes." I cry out.

"Oh, that's what I like to hear. Now, you're going to cum. Even when you are so sensitive and wishing that it will end. Trust me, smartass, it won't." His hands move across my exposed breasts, pinching my nipples and causing me to cry out. "pleasure can be a punishment too, sweet Ava. You're going to fucking cum until you pass out." I shake my head with tears in my eyes. "God, you look so pretty when you cry. It's a shame I will miss it."

He moves away from my body. "You look so fucking beautiful. Now cum for me like the bad fucking girl you are."

"Chase," I cry out. "Please—I've had—enough." I moan.

"Already? But we've just started." I shake my head. "Don't go anywhere now." He turns, walking towards the door.

"Please, please, please, oh god." I moan. "Please don't leave me." I cry, feeling tears drip down my cheeks.

"Oh, don't worry, baby, I will be back for the finale." He turns and walks away from me without another word.

"Come back," I squeeze out. "Oh fuck, make it stop," I scream into the empty room.

That bastard. He had left me here—like this. Oh god, the crawling pressure rushes through my body at an alarming rate. My pussy is pulsing with desire. My skin feels hot and my body shakes as the next orgasm rushes through my body. "Oh god, oh god, fuck, make it stop," I scream out as I feel my desire leak down my thighs.

He was trying to kill me; I was sure of it.

Death by orgasm.

The pleasure crashes through my body once more and I can feel the sheen of sweat pierce every part of my body and I'm not sure how much more I can take. My pussy is feeling numb as the vibrations move across me. Trembling, the pleasure takes over once more and I think I've lost the ability to scream, but I can still feel the impending orgasm that crashes through me once more.

Playing with Chase wasn't the adventure I thought it would be. Why couldn't I just leave the damn mask alone or shut my mouth when he had told me to? The pleasure rushes through my body and now my head feels muddy and black. I can't take anymore.

Please come back, please come back. I silently beg.

11

THE LIGHT TO MY DARK

CHASE

I can still hear her screams as I walk away from her. Fuck, she sounded fucking amazing. I wanted to turn back and sit and watch her move through every explosive orgasm as it overtook her pretty little body.

The way her face had blushed with the first orgasm had my cock pumping with desire and I wanted to forget about tor-turing her with orgasms and just play with her sexy little body but I knew she needed to learn her place and it wasn't what had poured out of that foul mouth of hers.

"What's the big emergency?" I ask Damon as I enter the underground bar, where we meet when there is an emergency.

"Oh, lover boy greeted us with his presence." He mocks.

"Don't start."

"Where were you last night?" He asks.

"Why are you so interested in my whereabouts?"

"Oh, I don't know, Casanova, we are being hunted and you keep disappearing."

"I didn't know you cared." I rolled my eyes because I knew better than to think his concern was care, there was something he wasn't telling me and I wasn't leaving until I found out what that was.

Looking around, I notice something is missing. In fact, two things were missing. "Where are Gage and Miles?"

"They are at home."

"Are you going to tell me what's going on?"

"The situation is a bit more complicated than you killing one of his men." That piqued my interest. "He said you have something valuable that belongs to him and if you give it back, he will forget the entire war and drop any animosity."

"What?"

"What does he think I've taken?"

"I was hoping you would tell me that."

"He didn't tell you?" He gives me a sympathetic look. "I took nothing from him. I thought losing Rossi was the reason for his vendetta."

"men are indispensable, but what you've taken from him—is priceless."

"Priceless?" The man who has everything thinks that something is priceless. Confusion crosses my face and I know he can see it because he holds the same expression that I do.

"You don't know, do you?" I look at him, hoping that he will put me out of my misery and just tell me what I don't know. "I think we should get a drink."

"I don't want a fucking drink."

"You'll need a drink. After what I found out, he sighs."

Walking back into Ava's estate, my heart is a little heavier than when I left. My obsession with Ava had grown over the months I had spent with her, I was going to let her go and now—well, now I didn't have a choice but first I would end her torture and give her what I knew she needed.

I hear her moans as soon as I climb the stairs. Interestingly, the little beast was still holding on. I had expected her to pass out from pleasure overload by now, but look at her, surprising me.

I stand by the door admiring the exquisite beauty that is Ava. Her body glistened with her sweat, spread wide, her body trembled as she pushed through another orgasm. I wondered how many she had gone through while I had been gone. A smirk falls across my lips. "Enjoying yourself?" I ask.

"Chase," she moans, "you bastard."

"Now, that's not very nice, is it?" I smirk.

"Please," she begs. "Please, make—it—stop. Oh my god, it's happening; again." She cries into the room.

Fuck, she's fucking soaked the bed. She's drowning in her own cum and she looks fucking delicious. I walk towards her. Her scent surrounds me and I tremble with desire as her scent surrounds me. I want to bask in her sweet scent and drown in her fucking soaking pussy.

"Please," she begs once more.

"Have you learned your lesson?" She nods. "So, you're going to be a good girl now?"

"Yes, oh god, yes, I will be good. I will be so good for you." She begs.

Walking towards her body, the tremors of desire slide up my spine. I shouldn't be in this room, not with her like this. Her scent is clouding my judgment. I just want to fucking ruin her little body. The sight of her squirming under her cum stained sheets will be forever etched in my memory.

My hand grips her ankles as I release her bound feet from the bed. "Oh, Chase, can't you? Fuck, please." She screams.

"What's wrong, baby?"

"Please, please, make it stop." She begs.

Sliding up her body, I feel her wet desire against my body and oh fuck, does it feel like the most delicious sensation? Her wetness, her scent. Fuck. I wanted it all. My hands slide up her thighs. "Oh god," she screams. "Please, please don't torture me." She cries.

"Oh, baby," I utter as I slide my hands further up her legs, teasing my fingers ever so close to her dripping pussy. "I haven't even begun to torture you," I whisper as I take the vibrator from her clit, giving her relief.

"Chase, Chase, please." She gasps as I see her cute little flushed face ride through yet another orgasm. I can feel her little body shake as she screams her release out and fuck me! The desire hits my body, and it feels like a truck just ran over me. I slide the vibrator out of her dripping pussy and throw it on the ground. "Why? Why did you wait so long?" She pants, relaxing her body.

"It would have been rude to interrupt you mid-orgasm. I'm not cruel, Ava. Even I want you to experience pleasure as it crashes over your body." My fingers dip inside her pussy. My God, so wet, so fucking ready. "And it was such a pretty sight seeing you soak your own bed with your delicious juices."

"Chase," she gasps. "Are you going to free me now?" Her bright blues beg me to free her. Her poor little hands must be numb by now. I can see the marks from the cuffs around her wrist and it gives me a shiver of excitement. Marked my beast, now she was mine. "Chase, please," she begs.

"Baby, now why do you have to open your pretty little mouth and ruin this moment?"

"Moment?" she screams. "Are you fucking crazy? You left me here for hours and now—." Scrunching up yesterday's knickers that still smell of her desire, I push the knickers to my nose and inhale. She displays a disgusted look on her face as I crawl over to her body and shove those panties in her mouth. I watch as she tries to move her head to spit them out, but without the use of her hands, the panties will stay there until I want to hear her scream.

"Oh, baby, look at you." I gasp as my eyes trail across her

delectable body. "Do you know how much I want you?" Her eyes widen, "So fucking beautiful." I wanted to devour her, fuck her until she bled and I would, but first I wanted to just feel her, every—fucking—inch.

Grabbing the coconut lotion, I lather it on my palms, feeling the smooth, cold consistency as I sit at her feet, pushing my hands up her little feet, adding pressure and moving my hands across them. I hear little murmurs come from her mouth. "Does that feel good, baby?" She nods her head. My hands move up her legs, massaging and rubbing in the lotion, feeling her tense legs relax beneath my touch. "You have gorgeous legs, Ava. They will look even prettier wrapped around my head." I gasp.

My hands move up her thighs, this time my fingers dig into her skin, leaving marks across her body, branding her as mine. I can hear the muffled cries as I work my way up her thighs until I'm so close to her sweet little pussy, but I move away from that, sliding my hands onto her hips and gripping tight of her. "You know who you belong to now, don't you?" I ask. She shakes her head. "You're mine, smartass." My fingers dig into her skin, drawing blood. "You've always been mine," I growl.

My hands crawl up her toned stomach, sliding my fingers across her delicate skin. God, she was so soft. Touching her made me feel things I had never thought I would feel again. My finger dips into her belly button, twirling because I wasn't missing a spot. I glide up to her chest, pushing my hands around her beautiful, voluptuous breasts and taking them in my hands. I squeeze and massage her, feeling her squirm beneath me. I pinch her nipples and pull hard until I hear her muffled cries once more.

My hands moved up to her shoulders, massaging and moving across her in a circular motion, adding pressure when I felt she needed it. kneading out all the tension I could feel. Her eyes rolled to the back of her head. She was enjoying this too much. My hand glides across her throat, sliding up and down until I grip her hard and shove my fingers into her mouth before removing the panties. "Now, be quiet or they go back in. Do you understand?" She nods her agreement.

My hand reaches between her thighs, feeling how fucking wet she is makes me shake with desire. I dipped my fingers inside of her to warm her up. One finger, she gasps. Two fingers, she's panting. Three fingers, she's moaning. She feels tight as fuck, but I'm still going to go further. Four fingers, her breathing is erratic, no words fall out, but her screams tell me it's too much. "See what a good girl you are, so full, so obedient, but I want to hear you fucking scream."

Sliding my fingers out, I make a fist. Poor little baby doesn't even know what's about to come. Pushing my enormous fist against her centre, I push forward, feeling her soaked pussy drip into my hand. Her eyes widen as my knuckles enter her. Tears are already streaming down her face. "Please, Chase, it's not—," Pushing my hand further, I force my entire fist inside of her. A loud scream falls from her throat and those tears just drip down her pretty porcelain face. Thrusting my hand harder and faster inside her, her screams fill the room, her body shakes, and I feel her push out all her desire against my hand.

Her body still shakes as I pull my hand out of her, her eyes wide and tears still fall. Her breathing is not regulating. I slide my hand across her face. "Breathe, you did so well, taking all of me. Such a good girl." I rasp.

She watches as I undress, her eyes widening once more. She didn't think her torment was over. I had smelt her, felt her and yet, I hadn't fucked her. Not the way I needed to, any-way. Crawling between her legs and positing my cock at her centre. "This might sting," I warn her as I push my cock deep within her dripping hole. She cries out and tears once again stream down her face. Reaching up, I uncuff her arms and give her the freedom to stop the ferocious fuck she was about to receive, but she doesn't even try.

She moves her arms across my neck and pulls me close. "It hurts," she cries. "It hurts so damn much." Her fingers dig into my back. "But don't stop." She moaned. "Don't fucking stop."

"Oh, I wasn't planning on stopping," I whisper. Forcing my body to crash against hers, I can feel every part of her as my cock moves inside of her. The pleasure crashes through every nerve in my body. Fuck. I don't want to stop. I want to fuck her just like this. Her legs wrap around my body, pulling me tighter against her.

My hips thrash against hers. Fuck. She feels so fucking good. I want to stay buried within her. This—this felt like home. My cock moves inside of her. I can feel the pulsing as the pleasure intensifies. Pushing her legs and wrapping them over my shoulder, I need to feel everything. All of her. Claim this little pussy as mine. She screams over and over once I hit her pussy as I deep as I can go. She's so fucking tight, so fucking wet, and yet I need more of her.

Grabbing her neck, I hold her in place, pinned to the bed by my cock. I feel her sink into the bed. Her screams hold no words. They are an incoherent mess; she struggling to scream, let alone speak. "Fuck. You're so fucking good, baby, so fucking good." I pound into her like her pussy is going to disappear. Her screams are louder, more painful. "Fuck me, you take my cock so well. So fucking well." I gasp.

She's fucking soaked my cock. It's a slippery mess down there, but it feels so fucking good. The pleasure crashes against me once more as my grip on her throat tightens. I can see the marks across her skin from how tightly I hold her in my hands. Thrusting harder and faster, I can feel my cock shudder from deep within me as I feel my cock explode and empty everything she had instilled inside of me into her pretty little dripping cunt.

I collapse against her body in a sweaty mess, panting against her skin. Tears still drip from her face. "I told you it would sting, baby." pulling out of her, I smile as I see my blood-smeared cock. Her bed is a mix of blood and cum, and it's the prettiest sight I've ever witnessed.

Moving away from her, I hold my hand out. "Oh god, what now?" She looks terrified. I can almost see the fear that moves across her face, but as she tries to take my hand, she cries out in pain.

"Stay there," I command.

"It's not like I can go anywhere, anyway." She responds.

I'm not gone long before I walk back towards her, carrying a bowl and placing it on the floor beside the bed. "Chase, I can't take anymore," she cries. "I can't—," I push a finger to her lips as I take the cloth from the bowl and slide it across her sore pussy. She gasps when the warm, wet cloth hits her pussy. "What—what are you doing?"

Sliding the cloth up and down her pussy and dabbing to ease her pain, I move and, giving her some comfort because once again I feel her relax. "I'm cleaning you up."

"But why?"

I shrug my shoulders as I continue massaging her pussy with the warm cloth, dipping it into the water. I wring it across her pussy and watch as the warm water splashes across her pussy. She hisses when the water first hits her, but after a while, she relaxes once as it soothes her.

Once I have bathed her and made sure that her pain is minimal, I crawl back onto the bed and take her in my arms. Stroking her hair and soothing her until she fell asleep in my arms.

This moment was bittersweet because when Ava woke up everything would be different. Everything would change and she would never look at me the same. She would never lay with me like this. This moment would never be the same. Soon she would hate me, hate the monster behind the mask, and what we shared today wouldn't matter to her, but for me, I could cherish it. I could remember it when she looked at me with hate.

Even if she couldn't appreciate the moment we were sharing right now, I would. I always would appreciate anything that I got from her. She was the light that lit up my darkness and as long as I could have a crack of light, I would know I was alive.

She stirs in my arms as morning breaks. I can hear her sweet groans in my ear as her eyes flutter open to look at me and a pretty little smile spreads across her face. I was wrong. The moment I thought I needed to keep wasn't her in my arms. It was this moment. Right now.

"Morning." She smiles.

"Morning. How do you feel?"

"A little sore, but satisfied." She smiles.

I hated myself. I hated myself for what I had to do. This was how it should have been ten years ago. Maybe she would have been my wife by now if she hadn't flitted into the night with my bank balance. Maybe things would have been different, but it wasn't. The gloominess of reality hit me and I was about to break her heart, just like she had broken mine.

It's what I thought I wanted. It's what I thought my goal was to hurt her just like she had hurt me, but as I look down at her flushed, smiling face, I don't want that. I don't want to hurt her. I don't want to break her heart. I knew if I did that, I would only break my heart.

My hand crawls across her face. "You are something special, Ava. Do you know that?" She screws her nose up at my comment. "Falling for you was my greatest adventure." I can see the tears welling in her eyes but I knew that feeling wouldn't last, her tears of happiness would soon turn to tears of sadness. "Why don't you get dressed?" I offer. She just smiles and moves from the bed. Leaving me all alone so the coldness could once again creep across my soul.

I watch as she slips the jeans across her tiny frame. Christ, even in jeans, she looked fucking delicious. She had curves to die for and I would die for her if it meant even for a moment; I had her heart. Once she's dressed, I walk towards her, slipping my arms around her waist as I hear her contented sigh. "I will always cherish our time together, sweet Ava."

She twists in my arms, turning to look at me with uncertainty displayed across her face. "Are you going somewhere?" I shake my head. "Then why does it feel you are saying goodbye?"

"This is not goodbye. This is more like—," I stroke her face one last time. "Hello,"

"Hello? I don't understand."

Moving away from her, I push my hands to the bottom of the mask. I knew the day would come when I would have to reveal my face, but I didn't think it would come so fast. It was supposed to be on my terms when I was ready. Oh, who was I fucking kidding? I would never be ready. Not for this. My fingers grip the bottom tightly and I push the mask from my face, letting it slip from my fingers and falling to the ground.

"Hello, little beast." Her face pales as she stands stiff, just staring into my eyes. I'm not sure if she remembers me, but she remembers the name I gave her while I was watching her.

"It was you." She gasps. "The whole time? It was you." I just nod. "Couldn't give me your name back then, but now, now you give me your name." She screams.

"You remember me?" I ask in shock.

"I wish I could forget." She whispers as tears fall down her face. "I wish I could forget everything."

"Ava." I reach out to touch her, but she moves away from me

like I've got a disease.

"Don't fucking touch me." She spits back at me. "Don't ever fucking touch me again." And just like that, the sweetness, the softness that I had experienced with Ava is gone and all that is left is hate. The hate I see burning within her eyes as she glares at me.

"Why?" she whispers. "Why?"

I run my fingers through my hair. "In the beginning, I wanted, well, I wanted, to get you back. What you did, I couldn't forgive and when I found out you were here, I just wanted to get revenge. Show you that every action has a consequence."

"Well, congratulations," she sniffles. "You got me. You made me believe you cared, but that was a lie. All you cared about was your stupid revenge." Tears stream down her face. The sadness that I wanted to avoid was staring me in the face.

"I don't care about that." I gasp. She turns her back on me. "I care about you." I scream out. She shakes her head and walks away.

I'm not sure why I'm surprised. What did I expect her to do, jump in my arms and forgive every horrible event I had put her through? Now, I was back to square one, alone with my obsession, and all that was left was the memory of her. The memory of what once was, but I knew that was a lie because our entire dynamic had been a lie.

Ava might hate me now, but she couldn't leave. I couldn't let her leave. Even if she hated me, she would understand, and one day she would understand. That what I did today. It was all for her.

Everything I had done was for her.

And I wouldn't apologise for that.

12

A BLAST FROM THE PAST

I thought he was my saviour, it turned out he was the evil that lurked in the shadows.

I wasn't sure what his name was. Darn, I never even possessed it. I was just a dumb kid. How was I meant to realize he would hold on to those feelings ten years later? Who even held onto something for that long? Psychos, psychos held onto something for that long, and he was a psycho.

I wanted to explain to him the reason behind my theft, but he wouldn't believe me. I could see it in his beautiful crystalline blue eyes when they looked at me with so much hatred.

I had never encountered a man as beautiful as him. When I saw him all those years ago sitting in the bar, of course, I was attracted to him. Who wouldn't be? That's not what caught my attention. It was the sadness that something shrouded him in. In a setting like this, it would seem that none of them owned a soul. It was like it carved them from the black abyss, spit out and just told to join human society, to fit in. Certainly, they presented themselves as normal, but upon closer scrutiny, the darkness entwining their souls was discernible.

He was different. There was something about the way he carried himself that intrigued me. That somewhere deep inside of this beautiful creature lay some humanity.

He talked little, but during our walk in the frosty night air, he did something unexpected. He displayed to me some kindness. I wanted to call it a night and leave with my dignity intact, but as I looked around, a sleek black vehicle followed me everywhere, watching my every move. I was aware I couldn't do that do that. It was him or me.

I hated myself for years. It burned the image of the man who had given me more in one night than anyone had given me my whole life into my brain. I wanted to make him aware that when he had given me that damn rose, but every time I opened my mouth, the words got caught in my throat.

What would I tell him, anyway? If I didn't take what was yours, Nikoli would kill me. He would end my miserable existence. I would have preferred to be dead, but after the kindness he had shown me, I saw a sliver of humanity had crawled across my soul. He had shown me kindness in a cruel, dark world and even though I knew what I had done to him was wrong but I would always remember him as the kind stranger that I kept locked in my heart, never to be seen again or that's what I thought.

Standing there looking back at the man I had held in my heart for all those years. He didn't look any different. I struggled to grasp the concept. He possessed a few lines that lay by his eyes, but other than that, he was still the same. Shrouded in sadness as he looked at me, the man who seemed so kind had tortured me to the brink of insanity, all to teach me a lesson. Something that I didn't even want to do. I understood that the repercussions from Nikoli would leave a lasting mark on my soul.

I walk away from him with his words lingering on my back. The words crawl across me, but all I can think of is lies. How was it possible for him to say he cared when he had done that, made me feel something for him? I trusted him, let him into my home, and he had done it all for revenge.

Now I was alone, but the threat I had feared all along had been living with me. The tears drip down my face at the realisation that he had in the end won. He got his revenge because he broke my heart. I had trusted him and now, in return, he had broken me.

When I get to the kitchen, Audrey is sitting there looking sullen with a cup of coffee in her hand. I stand there, awaiting the next surprise. She looks at me with a sympathy like she already knows, but how is it possible for her to know? How could anyone be aware?

"You knew." The words fell out of my mouth, surprising me more than her because they were too close. She brought him here. It was the only thing that made sense. Was she aware of everything? She must do because she's looking at me with guilt written across her face. "Audrey, speak to me," I shout louder.

"I knew." She whispers. "But he swore he just wanted answers. He swore he just wanted to teach you a lesson."

My shoulders slump. "That was ten fucking years ago, Audrey, ten years."

"I am aware." she sighs.

"You were supposed to be my friend." I gasp.

"I am your friend."

A chuckle falls from my lips as walk past her. "Ava, please don't leave. Not like this." I keep walking, "Ava," she screams.

"With friends like you, who needs enemies." I spit at her. "The apple doesn't fall far from the fucking tree." And I walk away. Away from the lie I had constructed, the friend I believed I could rely on, and the man I seemed unable to avoid.

I felt he would come for me. He wouldn't let me go, not now. It was impossible for him. He dug his claws deeper into me, and I still hadn't given him an answer. I knew that I was a coward. If I had just been honest with him, I could have solved it all, but I couldn't bring myself to do that.

I couldn't tell him about my painful past, but I also couldn't leave it out without letting him know I didn't want to hurt him. I didn't want to steal from him. I didn't want to leave him, but he wouldn't understand. Nobody would. So, I lived with my past, but my past discovered me and now I needed to escape.

I strolled through the clearing until I reached the forest, taking in the evergreen's scent woods that filled me with so much hope when I discovered this hidden little paradise. The paradise that transformed into my nightmare. I did not know where I was going. The only thing I comprehended was the need to keep going.

Shit. What did Audrey say? He tracks people. Well, I screwed up. How was I supposed to avoid a psycho with a mastermind's skill in tracking people? No, I wasn't able to think of that right now. If he found me, I wasn't sure what would happen, but I was sure I didn't want to find out.

Briefly looking back at the cherished home one last time. I can see him talking to Audrey from the window. Not as secluded as it seemed, everything from the forest was visible. Is this where he had hidden and watched me? God, how long had he been stalking me for? All this for money. I should have just offered to pay him back, but I was too upset when faced with the ghost of my past.

I shake my head as I take one last look at him before I turn away and get lost in the wildlife. The trees sway with the wind and if I wasn't in a hurry to get away from here, I would stand here and bask in the beauty that only nature could provide. The birds sing and chirp away like they are happy in their existence of being free. I wondered what that was like. Freedom. It was something I always battled for and never received.

Even when I managed to break free from Nikoli, it still felt like his prison held me captive. The power he possessed over me persisted for a lifetime. I knew he was still searching for me. So, how was it that a one-night stand gone wrong was the one who tracked me? I would prefer to be hunted by Chase than Nikoli. Nikoli was the evil incarnate and I would rather die than go back to him.

That's who I thought was stalking me. I thought he found me. I believed the nightmare I managed to escape from had resurfaced, but it wasn't Nikoli. It was the man I tricked. Not by my hand, but I'm not sure that's how he would look at it. Audrey always expressed that everyone was in control of their own choices. You just needed to decide which was the right choice, but I didn't believe that, not anymore.

I hear the crunch of the leaves beneath my feet as I walk through the forest, free, at least for now. The wind wraps around me like it wrapped me in its sweet embrace. I can now hear the stream of water as I approach the clearing into the next town over. As I rest by the stream, I let out a sigh while gently moving my fingers in the clear blue water, longing for a different life. I wished I didn't have to run, but knowing that I would always be running. Working towards creating distance between myself and my past. I'm on the run from the men who were hunting me. Escaping the clutches of my own thoughts.

Standing, I'm ready to make the journey to my new life I would have to create. Shit. Another new start. How many of these were I expected to start? How I yearned to be able to have a happy ending, but girls like me aren't able to achieve that. Plagued and shattered, the sole direction I possessed was a path of agony. The sole comfort I possessed was the understanding that I would be the one in control of this new beginning, with no Audrey or any other external forces. Just me.

"Little beast." I hear his voice and the shivers crawl up my back. How did he find me? I escaped the clearing, and he was already here. Some fucking fresh start this was.

I turn around, staring at him, looking into his cold blue eyes. Everything sounds silent, everything is still. Even the wind stills. It's as if the world came to a halt and enclosed us both at this moment. He doesn't move, but neither do I. It's like we are having a standoff. Who is going to make the first move? There is a sense of stiffness and strain. It's unusual because just a few hours ago, he was holding me in his arms, giving me a level of happiness I had never experienced before. I allowed my mind to wander that there was a possibility he might be the start of something amazing, but like everything else, it only left me disheartened and perplexed.

"Little beast," He sings once more. "You can run, Ava, but you can't hide." My brows furrow at his threat. "You have been running from me for so long, why not make it easier on yourself and just stop?"

Stop? Was he crazy? Well, I didn't need an answer to that. I knew he was. Why would I walk back towards him? I would have the confidence in knowing I gave it my all, even if he was going to catch me. All one can do in life is attempt to do their best.

"Why would I want to do that?" I smirk, almost taunting him.

"You're just prolonging the inevitable."

"Maybe? But I would rather run from you than let you feel you earned some self-gratifying victory by making me obedient. I'm not yours and I won't be."

"You are mine." He growls. "When I catch you, little beast, you'll wish you had chosen the easy way." I gulp because the fire in his eyes tells me that his words are not lies. "So, what's it going to be?"

13

NIKOLI BELVEDERE

AVA

I stood as a mere child when I encountered Nikoli. It is always those who pretend to be the Saviour that becomes your undoing. I believed he bore a resemblance to the father figure I never encountered. In the beginning, it seemed like he wanted to help me. I could make-believe that his eyes didn't dwell on my body for an excessive duration because he presented me with something I didn't have - he offered me a family or what I imagined a family to be.

I felt grateful for the home he provided me, but nothing comes for free in this world.

How could I possibly know that I had just made a deal with the devil.

Sitting on the streets where I belonged, no family to turn to. It was a sorry state to be in at only fourteen years of age. I would cry, but I don't think I had any tears left. There wasn't even any shelter. The rain pounded down, and if I didn't die from pneumonia, perhaps I would die from loneliness.

I didn't think you could die from a broken heart because if you could...I would already be dead.

The tears fall down my face, but I'm not sure you'd notice with the torrential rain that pounded down in the night's dead.

"Now, why does a pretty young thing like you look so sad?" I hear his thick Irish accent. With rapid eye movements through my tears and the rain, my head raises to meet his cold blue eyes. "Hello darling, what are you doing out here alone? You'll catch your death."

"One can only hope." I utter through the tears that still fall.

"Why aren't you at home?" He asks, but I don't answer. Apart from anything else, everything inside of me is screaming for me to RUN, but I don't. I sit there looking up at the stranger, trying to assess his intentions.

He brushes his hand across the stubble on his face. "Oh, you don't have a home." He speaks out loud as if he's just had an epiphany. "You know, I have a daughter about your age." I squint my eyes at him. "I'm sure you will get on great. Would you like to meet her?"

I should've said no. I should've placed my trust in my intuition. That's what it was there for, right? To warn you of situations likes this.

"I can give you a hot meal and a warm bed for the night." The sick feeling turns around my stomach the moment those words leave his lips. "I promise you'll be quite safe. I won't let anyone hurt you. If you come home with me, you'll always be safe."

The queasy sensation remains, but it seemed he had no plans to leave either. "I understand you don't trust me, but I can't leave you out here alone. I would never forgive myself if something happened to you." He holds out his hand. "So you'll be doing me a favour." He smiles.

Sensing nothing but coldness creep across my soul as he takes my hand and pulls me to my feet. "What's your name, little darling?"

I half contemplated giving him a fake name, but why would I need to do that? I was just an orphan, down on her luck. "Ava," I mutter.

He shakes my hand. "Nice to meet you, Ava. I'm Nikoli."

Nikoli wasn't the friendly man I had first thought he was. I had spent many nights crying in my room. I wish I had a time machine so I could go back. Go back to that night when I should have said no. It was impossible for me to foresee what he had planned for me.

The first few years were a breeze, and the estate that I now called home was exquisite. It was a beautiful colonial building that housed the most expensive art; I loved looking upon the great masterpieces from artists long gone. It evoked a sense of nostalgia for places I had never seen. I had met Audrey that first night; she was everything he said she was and when they were done with me; she was the one who would come to my room to console me.

He said nobody would hurt me, but that was a lie.

I was sixteen when Nikoli came to my room one night. I remember it because it was the night it dashed forever, my hope that decent people existed in this world. My door opens. I should have pretended to be asleep, but I'm unsure if that would have deterred him. Nikoli took what he wanted and when he had it, he deemed it as his. As he owned you, he often told me how I was his most prized possession, but I wasn't an object. That always confused me, but I would find out that's all I was, his possession that he owned. That he could do what he wanted with. A possession that he would never let go.

He sits on the edge of my bed. I notice the bed moving beneath me as he occupies the space. In a slight incline, he sweeps my long hair aside and stares at me in the dimness. The identical gaze I had strived to avoid as time went on. His eyes always had lingered a little too long on my body, but I had ignored it. He had saved me, after all. Why would he want to hurt me?

"You've grown into a beautiful young woman, Ava." I say nothing. "I've waited two years. I didn't have to. I have shown you kindness by resisting you." He was saying things I didn't understand. He pulls the covers from my body and coldness creeps across me and it's not from the room—it's from him. "Now, let me have a look at you."

His eyes trail across my body, and I see his tongue flick across his lips. I wasn't sure if he needed a drink, but common sense told me not that. Not that at all. As I become aware of his hands moving across my breasts, brushing against my nipples, I know this is wrong. It doesn't feel right. "Please, don't," I beg him.

"Shhhh, don't worry, little Ava, I won't hurt you." His fingers move across the vest, brushing across my nipples until they form into hardened peaks. "Oh, good, very good." He gasps. His hands crawl down my body, lifting the vest over my head until I'm lying there with no top on. Quivering because of the cold and my understanding of what is going to take place

in this room.

He runs his fingers all the way down my stomach until they are hooked beneath the band of my shorts. I shake my hand, but once again; he promises he won't hurt me as he drags my shorts and panties from my body. His eyes light up as he sits there just looking at me, exposed for him.

He spreads my legs and I'm helpless to do anything. All I can do is watch him and hope that he comes to his senses and stops, but I'm not that naïve. I know he will not stop. He's been waiting for this. "So pretty, such a pretty girl." He smiles. His fingers move between my legs, and I can feel him rubbing my pussy at first, "please don't," I cry. "Please stop." This doesn't make him stop, this causes him to rub faster. My breath is erratic, and a sensation travels through my body that I can't grasp. "That's it." He gasps. Faster and faster, he rubs my pussy. I sense a sudden jolt of electricity traveling through my body, and then something unusual takes place. I feel wet. "Oh god, yes." He moans. "The next one will be better."

The next one? I had thought this horrendous experience would be over but I was soon going to find out I was in for a long gruelling night with Nikoli, he may have waited two years but he would make up for it with the horrific acts he displayed on my once innocent body.

He spreads my legs wider, looking down as he looks where he had just been touching me. "You never touched yourself before?" I shake my head. "Did that feel good?" Once again, I shake my head. "It didn't?" He displays a confused look on his face. "The first one is always the worst one." Somehow, I doubted that. Grabbing my knees, he spreads my legs wide. "You look so beautiful, my pretty little girl." He sighs as his eyes look between my legs. "You are the best thing I ever found."

"Nikoli, please," I beg. "You don't need to do this. We can forget this ever happened. Please don't do this."

"Silly girl. I want to do this." His fingers move across my pussy, and I feel shame when a moan falls from my throat. "Ah, there you go now. It feels good. I'm going to make you feel even better." I shake my head. I feel a finger enter me and my body fails me once more. My back arches and gasps fall from my lips. "Yes, that's it, my pretty little girl. You cum for me." I shake my head. But his finger twirls inside of me, making my body feel alive, pushing me to the edge before a scream falls from my lips and once again the slick wetness crawls out of my body.

"You cum so fucking good for me." He mutters. He rubs my inner thighs before he spreads my legs as wide as they can go. "That's right, you open up for me." I'm not sure what else he could do, but then I see his head dip between my legs. I feel his hot tongue glide up and down my pussy and I feel ashamed because I don't want this. I know I don't want this, but it feels good in a bad way. His mouth comes down hard against me and his tongue enters me, thrashing around. "Oh god," I cry out. "Please—fuck, please." His fingers move across my clit faster and faster while his tongue massages me. "Oh—my—god," I scream. "Nikoli, no, stop, it's wrong." I cry with tears crawling down my face. A rush of heat and desire spreads across my body. His tongue flicks deep inside of me. My hands push his head into my pussy as I scream out, feeling my legs tremble. The whoosh of wetness thrashes out harder and faster this time.

His head comes up and I see him lick his lips. "I knew you'd be delicious. My pretty little girl. See, that wasn't so bad, was it?" My body shakes and tears fall down my face as I sob. He moves up my body, his hands moving across my breasts, pinching my hardened nipples. "So, young. So ripe. All mine." He smiles. "You feel so good. Now stay still, pretty girl." I watch as he undresses. "Please Nikoli, please don't do this." He never says a word as he lays his body across mine. "I know I said I wouldn't hurt you." Fear shoots up my spine. "But this part hurts everyone, at least for the first time around."

He kneels between my legs, holding his hard cock and moving closer and closer to my body. I attempted to squirm away because of my awareness of what was about to happen, but he held onto my hip. "Stay still, Ava. I don't want to hurt you, but I will." He threatens. My body stills. "Good, that's good." He smiles. He pushes his cock at my centre and I want to die. The pain as he pushes his cock into my body hits me. I can feel a burning sensation and I cry out when he pops inside of me. "Fuck, such a tight little virgin." He gasps. He thrusts on top of me, and the friction of his penis stings with each movement. At first, his movement is slow, but when I pant, he speeds up. Burying his nails into my skin. I close my eyes and pretend I'm not here, that this isn't happening, but with each thrust, a moan falls from my throat, causing him to move deeper and faster with every breath I give. "Yes, that's it, my pretty girl." He cries out. "Fuck, yes, cover me in your cum." The pleasure from his act moves through me once more and I can't help the screams that fall from my lips. "Fuck, yes, my little Ava, fuck." He cries and I can feel him pour his desire inside of me.

When he finishes, he says nothing. He just puts his clothes back on and leaves as if he was never in there to begin with. I have no words for what he's done. I just lay there with blood smearing my thighs. The man who I thought saved me had just taken away the only thing that was mine to give and he wanted me to be grateful. I hated him.

I curl up in a ball, and I cry. I'm not sure why tears won't solve anything. Now he knew he could do it, I knew he would do it again. He didn't want to save me; he wanted to use me and own me. That was his plan all along.

Every night was the same. I learned to not tell him to stop because after a while I said those words he would hit me hard across the face and I was powerless to do anything but take his beating. He had trained me to be whatever he wanted me to be. I was trapped with no way out.

When I hit twenty, Nikoli was in his element. I was the bait for every poor schmuck he deemed owed him. I would get sent to bars all over New York and all I had to do was get them so drunk that when they fell asleep, I would transfer their funds to Nikoli's account. Simple. Nobody would ever suspect that a sweet young woman would con them.

I wasn't permitted to have sex with any of them, just gave the illusion that I would have sex with them. I belonged to him and Nikoli didn't like to share his toys. The night I met Chase, something changed inside of me. Sure, I broke the rule by sleeping with him, but his one act of kindness saved me.

A week later, I was free. Free from the life I had been subjected to and free from Nikoli. I never thought his daughter would go through with it, but any tears I had cried, she had cried them right with me. She, of course, played her role well and acted sad when I was gone, but unbeknownst to her bastard father, she knew where I was all along.

Every day I lived in fear, fear that one day he would catch up with me. One day, he would find me and I would once again endure a life that no longer belonged to me. I had stayed undetected for ten years, but somebody had found me. I thought it was Nikoli, but it wasn't.

It was the man who had saved me.

14

YOU CAN RUN BUT YOU CAN'T HIDE

CHASE

I give her time to leave. She wanted to run let her run. This didn't show that I wouldn't catch her. It meant I was giving her a head start. Let her believe she escaped me. I could not release her, even if I desired to. I wasn't the only one hunting her. Nikoli knew I was here with her. He had found her. She was the priceless item I possessed, and he desired her to be given back.

I knew little about the history of Nikoli and Ava. Audrey

would never give me details. All she had told me was if her dad got his hands on Ava again, he would kill her and I couldn't have that.

Upon hearing Damon's words, my heart sank. Shit. It never crossed my mind that I possessed a heart, but upon discovering who was after her, my chest felt the sting of pain. It was at that moment I realized that perhaps the little beast meant more to me than I cared to admit. Sure, in her eyes I would be the monster and I would let her believe that as long as I could keep her safe.

I wait a little while. Being in a spot in her room where I saw her from the forest. If my obsession with getting close to the little beast hadn't been so strong, she might still be hidden from sight. He would have never found her if I had just let her go, but I couldn't do that. I wanted her to tell me why and after a while; I wanted to make her mine, but now, now, that didn't seem possible. I'm sure Nikoli only existed to fuck up my life.

I sigh as I walk down the stairs and see Audrey sitting there, looking rather sullen. "Where is she?" I'm not sure why I was asking because I already knew the answer. Ava would've left after she fled from me—once again.

"She's gone." She mutters. "She hates me." Tears spill down her face.

"She doesn't hate you." I try to reassure her. "She's just—she's angry."

"She thinks I betrayed her." She swirls the liquid in her cup and keeps her eyes down. "She will never forgive me for what I have done."

"Yes, she will."

She raises get head to look at me. "She's gone, Chase. Ava has gone."

"Oh, don't worry, she won't get far," I smirk.

I turn to walk away to search for the little beast. I granted her a sufficient period to establish an early lead on her brief runaway adventure. "Chase," I turn my head and look back at her. "Why don't you just let her go?"

Those words caused a shooting pain to hit my body. The idea of never witnessing her beautiful, innocent eyes brimming with vitality caused a chill to crawl over my body. I shake my head. "I can't do that." I mutter as I walk into the frosty night air.

As I step into the forest, nostalgia washes over me. This is where it all began, how poetic that this is where it would conclude. She walks. I spot her hiding behind a tree. Why isn't she running? She's wandering around as if she's unaware that I'll go searching for her, but Ava isn't that clueless. She knows I will come after her. Isn't it the reason her head twists, in search of any signs of life, and then she does something that causes my heart to flutter? She sits by the stream, sliding her fingers through the clear water. She looks so innocent. I wait until she stands before I come out from the trees.

"Little beast," I call out to her. I can see the stiffness in her back and she turns like there is imminent danger in the area. I would never hurt her. Hasn't she realized this yet? I longed to set her free. No, it wasn't true, but I would've allowed her to go. I will allow her to begin a fresh chapter in a different location where she was a stranger, if that's what would bring her happiness, but as long as Nikoli remained alive, I couldn't make that choice. I couldn't let her go.

"Little beast," I call out to her once more. "You can run, Ava, but you can't hide." Confusion hits her body like she didn't know I would find her. "You have been running from me for so long, why not make it easier on yourself and just stop?"

"Why would I want to do that?" She lets a smirk display across her lips and it takes everything I have not to smile back at her because that fire, that fire that had been missing, was back and lit her up from the inside out.

"You're just prolonging the inevitable," I warn.

"Maybe? But I would rather run from you than let you feel you earned some self-gratifying victory by making me obedient. I'm not yours and I won't be."

Oh, that was not the right answer. Not mine? She was fucking mine. She was mine then, and she was mine now. Why would I chase her if she wasn't mine? Ava might despise me with every ounce of fight she had remaining in her body, but I would still claim her. I would make her realize she was always mine.

"You are mine," I growl. "When I catch you, little beast, you'll wish you had chosen the easy way." I looked at her with determination because if she didn't believe my words, she would see the honesty in my eyes. "So, what's it going to be?"

She stands there, determined. Her back straight, holding that fire within her soul and showing me that the fight she held within her was still present. "Catch Me if you can." She smirks. She turns and starts running.

Run, little beast run.

Walking towards the stream, I look down at the spot where she was. What did she see that made her stop? I would never understand it, but Ava seemed to view the world differently. When I walked through this forest, it provided an easier path to walk undetected, but Ava appreciated the view she found herself in. Oh, how I wish I could view the world through her eyes.

Who would have thought it? She surprised me? It was something I didn't see coming. When I challenged her to give up, it wasn't because I wanted her to, since the chase made up for half the fun. She knew she would end up in my arms. She would end up with me, but then something sparked in her dazzling eyes, mischief.

I knew I was living on borrowed time and that I shouldn't play with her in the forest but when she had challenged me, taunting me to catch her. I knew I wanted to play with her. Despite the imminent threat, I desired to capture the little beast, and it excited me that she wouldn't make it easy for me.

I can hear her breath as I take long strides. She never strays from the straight path we traveled on. Well, this didn't prove to be much of a challenge. I could smell the essence of her floral perfume as I walked through the forest, picking up the pace, getting desperate to catch the little beast.

It had been a long time since I had tracked anything. However, I hadn't found anything as delicious as the little beauty I was hunting.

Like a wolf catching it's prey and this wolf was hungry.

RUN, LITTLE BEAST, RUN

AVA

I run faster and faster, my heart rate picks up as I speed through the trees. I could no longer see him, but I knew he wasn't far behind me.

Taunting him was fun because I knew once he caught me I was in trouble. My breath is ragged as I lean against a tree.

"Oh, Ava, I can fucking smell you." I hear him call. Shit. I knew he wasn't far behind me. "When I catch you, little beast,

I'm going to fuck you." Shit. That should terrify me, but it doesn't. The only emotion his words cause is excitement.

My breathing is erratic as I push my body to move away from the tree, running forward to get away from the hunter that was on the prowl. "Oh, little beast, keep fucking running. It only excites me more." Shit. The desire crawls up my thighs as I feel my feet pound on the ground. Faster and faster I run, my heart is beating so fast I'm not sure how long I can keep up the pace.

I no longer hear him as I lean over, holding my side as a shooting pain shoots up my side. Great, that's all I need. A stitch in my side. Just breathe, I tell myself as I try to regulate my breathing. I had run fast and far. There was no way he could have caught up with me yet. I just needed a moment to recover. I can feel the sweat dripping down my back. Standing tall, I hold my side as I steady myself, ready to once again run away from the maniac who was hunting me.

I try to move forward, but I'm pulled back to the spot I stood in. Chills hit my body when I feel his warm breath on my neck. His grip on the back of my neck yanks my body harder until I plummet against his body. "I would have let you keep running—." He breathes into my ear. "But, little beast, I just couldn't wait to catch my prize." I try to struggle out of his grip, but anytime I struggle, he grips me harder until I yelp. "I humoured you and let you leave once." His teeth nip at my ear. "That won't be a repeat performance."

"Let me?" I let out a nervous laugh. "You really are full of yourself, aren't you?"

"Oh, little beast, that smart mouth of yours will land in a world of trouble." I roll my eyes. He loosens the grip on my back and I twist to face him, but once I look into his eyes, I wish I could turn back around. His eyes look at me with raw intensity and I can feel the blush creep up my cheeks within moments. God, why does he have this effect on me? "Oh, look at you. So pretty, so pink. Even now, you want me to touch you." I shake my head. "No?" He whispers. "I tell you what if you're not fucking soaking for me then I won't touch you but if you are—," He raises a brow, his hands slide down my body, his hand dips into my jeans dipping into my panties and I let out a moan once his fingers hit my pussy. "Oh, little beast, you're in fucking trouble." He smirks.

His large hand wraps around my throat and if I don't cum from this act alone. I try to hold in the moans that are dying to squeeze from my throat, but it doesn't last long. He throws my body to the ground, still holding me by the throat. "Let me go, Chase." I strangled out the words.

"Not a fucking chance, baby." His lips crash hard against mine. I want to sink into the delicate darkness that is swirling around my body, but I raise my hand and slap him across the face. He lifts his head and darkness swirls in his crystal-blue eyes. "Oh, baby, you are going to regret that." He threatens. His other hand grips my wrists. I try to struggle from his hold, but his grip is too tight to even move. He holds my arms above my head and I try to wriggle from beneath him. His lips once again crash against mine, and once more the dark taste of Chase has my body in knots, his tongue wrestles against mine in an erotic burst of pleasure. "I have been dying to taste you." His tongue slides across my lips and a desperate moan crawls from my throat. "For fucking months." He growls.

His hand moves from my throat, but it still feels like I can't breathe. His scent, his body. It feels like I'm breathless with nothing but seduction whirling around my head. I can feel his hands crawl down my body as he drags the jeans and panties from my body. "Chase," I beg.

"Baby, you never learn." He gasps, "That smart mouth of yours is begging for this." I shake my head. "No?" He spreads my legs apart with his thighs. "No matter what I do to you, I forbid you to cum." My eyes widen. "You will not get a release until I think you deserve one."

"You can't be serious," I laugh.

"Oh, I'm very serious." He holds a serious expression on his face to let me know he is not joking. Not that I ever thought he was. If there was one thing I knew about Chase, it was he wasn't much for telling jokes.

His fingers dip into my dripping pussy and the moans crawl from my throat almost immediately. "Hold it." He instructs. I shake my head. His fingers twirl deep inside of me. "One, don't you dare fucking cum." His fingers slide deeper inside of me, moving faster. "Two, keep holding it." His fingers hit me hard and fast. My breathing is erratic as the moans crawl out of my throat. "Three, you're going to cum so hard for me—but not yet." He breathes. His fingers curl and move at a faster pace, pushing my body to heights I've never felt before, faster and faster as his fingers move inside of my dripping pussy. The screams crawl from my throat and his fingers eject from my pussy.

As I try to catch my breath, my eyes widen from the shock. "I told you, you are not going to cum until I tell you to. Now, we have to start again." I shake my head. "You only need to make it to the count of ten."

"But you count so slowly." I wail.

"Oh, do I?" He smirks. "I hadn't noticed."

"Chase, you made your point."

"I don't think I did. You haven't felt the desperation that you should be feeling right now."

"Desperation," I repeat as I blink into his intense eyes that seem to undress me with every dark look that passes across his face.

His finger entered me once more. "One, don't you dare cum." He counts again. His fingers push deeper and I can once again feel the burst of electricity shoot through my body. "Two, hold it." His fingers curl and hit that oh-so fucking sweet spot. I have to bite my tongue to not let the growing orgasm release from my body. "Three, your body is dying to release, but you're not going to cum until I tell you to, are you?" I shake my head, unsure if that is a lie or not. "Good Girl," His dexterous fingers glide further inside of me, curling and pressing that sweet spot that has the moans crawling from my throat. "Four, you're so close now, but you're going to be a good girl for me and hold off just for a little longer." His fingers move faster and faster and the moans turn to screams. "Five, that desperation is crawling through your body, baby. The only thing you can think about is cumming for me—but not yet." He teases.

I'm fucking soaked. He wasn't wrong. All I can think about is the release that keeps building and building but never ends. This was actual torture. I was no longer thinking about running. In fact, I wasn't thinking at all. The only thoughts that ran through my head were how desperately I needed to release all that desire across his fingers. The knot in my stomach was almost unbearable and the dizzy feeling that had overtaken my brain with the intense need to just let go was more than I thought I could handle.

"Please, please let me cum." I beg him.

His fingers move faster and faster. I can feel my legs shake at the impending desire that threatens to pour out of me—at last. And then he stops, and that frustration hits my body in waves. "You fucking bastard." I cry out. He just smiles at me, "Please, I need to cum." I plead.

His fingers resume their movement inside of me once more, and the pleasure that had been paused hits my body faster this time. Screams rip from my throat and I'm so fucking close. "Six, don't fucking cum or we will start all over again." My eyes widen at his words and I try to focus on holding off the orgasm that wants to rip through my soul like a demon.

The way he looks at me causes my body to curl with desire. I shouldn't want this, after everything, I shouldn't want this, but the way he's looking at my has all sense falling out of my empty head. All I can think of is the release that he just won't give me. "Seven, I can see the desperation in your eyes." His head moves closer to mine. "But you just don't seem desperate enough." He whispers. Tears pool in my eyes, threatening to fall as his fingers push as deep as they can go, pushing me closer and closer to the edge. "Hold it," He instructs.

"I can't, I can't." I cry as fresh tears spill down my cheeks, more out of frustration than anything else. My body is on edge, the tremors shoot through my body like electricity is travelling through every nerve in my body. "Please, please stop tormenting me." I cry out.

"You can." His fingers move faster and faster and I can feel the pleasure building faster and higher. "And you will." He's moving so deep inside of me I can take any more torture from his delicious movements. "Eight, Oh, you're doing so good, baby. Doesn't it feel nice being so close to the edge?" I shake my head. Faster and faster the desire crawls through me. "Nine, you are so close now, desperate for release. Each one stronger than the last. You are going to cum so hard for me."

He picks up the speed, the screams rip from my body, and the crawling desire hits me like I'm wrapped in a vortex. I no longer know where I am. All I know is the pleasure he's forced upon me creeps up on me and hits me in places I've never felt before. "Ten," He gasps. "Cum for me, baby, cum for me so fucking hard." He growls. My body shakes before he even finishes that sentence. The screams run through me and my body shakes with a desire that just won't stop. The desire bursts out of my body in an explosive mass of desire.

He looks down at me and the bastard fucking smirks at me. He smirks at me. I would scowl if I had the energy, but all I can do is try to regulate my breathing. The swirling vortex has settled in my brain, but this doesn't feel unwelcome, more like pleasure has settled and I'm satisfied. "Don't get comfortable, baby, I'm not done with you yet." My eyes widen. What more could there be? After, after that explosive rush of desire that had ripped through my soul.

He removes the rest of my clothes from my body. I squint at him, unsure why he's removing my clothes in the forest. He places a choker around my neck with a bell tied to it. I roll my eyes, "What am I, a cat?" I mock him.

"Oh, Ava, being a smart ass won't help you."

"Chase, give me my clothes back."

"No." He states. "Here is what is going to happen, little kitty. You are going to run." I look at him. "When I catch you, I will take my prize and fuck you." He smirks.

"You expect me to run in the forest. Naked with no shoes on." I glare at him.

"Well, you aren't naked." He smiles while running his finger across the choker he has placed on my neck.

"Oh yes," I roll my eyes, "A bell to alert you to my movements. How generous."

"I will count to ten—."

"Oh," I smile. "You'll never catch me if you count as slow as you did when you were torturing me."

"Oh, don't worry, baby, I will catch you." He holds a stern look, with desire swirling in his eyes. "Now, run." My eyes run across his face to assess if he's been serious or not, but as I look at him, there is not a glimmer of amusement. Shit. He was very serious.

Clambering to my feet, I just stand there, shivering, as I cast my gaze back at him. I know what I'm supposed to do but I also don't want to give him the satisfaction and if by some miracle I could get away from him. I was naked. Where would I go with no clothes on? "What are you waiting for?" He questions me. "Run." turning almost in a robotic motion, I try to hold in the gasp as I feel the rough mud and twigs beneath my bare feet and start sprinting at a steady speed with the distant sound of his voice counting behind me.

My feet crush against the hard ground and I can't help feeling how cruel he is that he would make me run through the forest once more with nothing on my feet. I can sense the cold pimples rise across my body as the biting wind nips at my skin. I can't stop even though the biting cold slows me down. I no longer hear his counting, so I must have moved far enough ahead of him. The jangle from the chain sounds with every movement like a big warning sign to alert him to my location.

Rushing forward, my breath becomes ragged, and the cold hits my body, causing my body to shake and wobble. I turn my head to the side as I run, but I can't see anything. Exhaling in relief, my body collides with something solid. In the beginning, I presumed I had run into a tree until I detected his robust arms enveloping my body. "Well, little beast, that wasn't much of a challenge."

Raising my eyes, I meet his. The smug expression is clear on his face as he gazes down at me. My breathing is erratic as I lean against his body, trying to get my breath back. "How—how did you get here so fast?" I gasped out. "But you were all the way over there. How?" I ask in disbelief.

"When will you learn?" He pokes my nose and I wriggle my nose in response. "I always win." He smiles.

"You are way too cocky." I smile. "You know what they say, Chase, that is when you are about to lose." Raising my knee, it connects with his side. I see a grimace pass across his face and I wriggle out of his grip as I turn to run in the opposite direction. I sense his arms enveloping my waist once more, pressing my body against his. "Nice try, baby. I already won."

I hit against his chest, but he doesn't even flinch. "Keep fighting me, I like it." The arrogant asshole grins at me and the rage crawls through my body at the thought of him thinking I'm some sort of prize that he had won. Well, he wouldn't be getting a reward for his cruelty. Not this time. "I see that determined look in your eyes, Ava, deny it all you want. You want this—you want me." A blush creeps across my body. "I wonder if your pussy is blushing for me too, baby." He whispers.

"Chase, you are an arrogant asshole. I wouldn't want you if humanity depended on it. I would rather the world disintegrate into nothing than give you the satisfaction—." His lips crash against mine and I sink into his delicious dark, intoxicating taste before I come to my senses. Raising my hand, I crash my palm against his face. "What do you think you are doing?" I scream.

His hand crawls to my face and the entire world stops. Everything just stops. It's like I'm on a merry-go-round that has paused. Time stood still as he gazed into my eyes, bringing his face closer to mine. "I want to taste the anger on your lips. It's mine, little beast, it's all mine." He utters before his lips crash against mine and pulls me into the darkness that sucks me in like a vortex. "Your anger is delicious, baby. You still taste like fucking sunlight." He gasps. My brows knit in confusion. "My little light." He smirks as he throws me to the ground.

"I'm not yours." I speak as I watch him undress. I could have scrambled to move, but I just lay still, mesmerised by his body. My eyes trail over every curve, every muscle. My mouth is watering. The tattoos that crawl up and down his arms appear like art. The crawling Dragon that is inked across his chest is deadly but beautiful. Much like Chase, deadly but beautiful. I shook my head. This man was dangerous, and I needed to get as far away from him as I could, and yet I didn't budge, not even an inch.

He crawls across my body, pinning me to the ground. "You are mine and if all you have for me is hate. Well, little light, I will burn within your hate and taste every drop so it burns through my soul and leaves yours." My mouth opens. I want to speak, but his words hit me and warmth spread across my body. "You are much too beautiful to carry hate in this perfect little body. So, I will take it all and let your hate consume me. If that's all you'll give me, I want it all." He growls down my ear.

"Chase," I have no words. I gasp his name before he's even touched me. I want to fight him, show him I'm not the weak little girl he seems to view me as but laid in his arms, those words that spread warmth to my body holds me frozen to spot. Frozen in time, allowing his words to swallow me and swirl across my body. His fingers glide up my thighs, spreading my legs so that he can nestle between them. "Chase," I gasp once more.

"Oh baby, are you practising?" His fingers glide between my legs, sliding across my pussy. "Oh, baby, you are already fucking wet for me. So fucking ready for me." I scowl, but then I feel his fingers enter me and my back arches in response as the pleasure hits me and the moans fall from my lips. "You might hate me, Ava, but your fucking pussy loves me." He gasps.

"Chase, fuck, you—I—I don't; fuck, yes, just—like—that," I scream out, feeling the desire rush through me as his fingers work my body like a musician playing his favourite instrument. "Why are you so fucking good at that?" I cry out as his finger curls even further inside of me.

His fingers move out of me and I watch as his thick tongue slides out of his mouth, sucking all of my desire from his fingers, groaning each time he tastes me on his tongue. His eyes roll into the back of his head like it's the most delicious meal he's ever tasted. "Fuck, baby, you taste—so fucking good." He rasps. His mouth comes down against my peaked nipple and the moans fall out fast. I experience his tongue encircling me, taking me between his teeth, pulling and sucking until the sharp shooting pains transform into pleasure. "Oh, baby, I love how you respond to me." He smiles before he bites down hard on my nipple, causing shooting pains to travel up my spine and screams to rip from my body. "God, even when you bleed, you're delicious." His tongue slides across my nipple. "Don't worry, baby, I will kiss you better." He places his lips across my nipple, kissing my nipple where he's broken the skin.

My fingers dip into his shoulder blades. "Fuck, Chase." I cry out. I feel him press his hard cock against my pussy, sliding up and down my soaking wet pussy, causing my body to shudder with delight. "Oh god, yes, please don't stop." I cry out. His hard cock hits my clit with every movement he makes against me. The pleasure crawls through my body, but it's not enough. I want more. More of him. Just more.

His cock moves harder and faster between my pussy lips. I can hear the squelch of my wetness as he moves against me. "Fuck. Your pussy juice all over my cock is my favourite scent. God, baby, I want to wear you—every—fucking; day." He moans. His moans cause my pussy to pulse with desire. Every deep groan has my pussy clenching with desire. I feel him push his cock deep inside of my hungry, pulsing pussy. "Fuck. Ava, you're fucking squeezing the life out of me." He gasps. "Shit, why does your pussy feel so damn good?" He curses as he pushes deeper inside of me. The moment his cock thrusts deeper inside of me, I see stars. This man has my body exploding like a firework within seconds. The pleasure rushes through my body and I feel alive.

Grasping the back of my head, I can detect him tugging my hair, resulting in a blazing sensation on my scalp. The intense sensation brings about a burning feeling as it moves down my spine. His hips bang against mine as he fucks into my body like he's starved for it. The way my body shudders with every penetrative thrust has screams ripping through my body. My nails dig into his skin, but it still doesn't seem enough as I claw at his skin. "Oh god, yes, fuck. You're—so—fucking; good." I scream. My pussy throbs around him, experiencing the intense sensation of his cock. He thrusts harder and faster. I can almost feel him in my belly, like he's trying to crawl into my body and render me under his spell.

"Fuck, Ava, fuck me." He gasps. "Cum for me, baby, cum for me." He pleads. I'm not sure how much longer I can hold on as the burst of desire overtakes my body. Trembling with desire as the pleasure tears through my soul. A scream that doesn't even feel like it comes from me rips from my throat and I hold on to his wet skin and drench his cock in the desire he had ripped from my body. "Fuck. That's it, baby, fucking soak my cock." He cries out. I feel his cock jerk hard deep inside of me. The grip on my hair tightened, leaving a buzzing sound to crawl around my brain as I heard his loud grunts of approval pour from his lips as I felt him pump strand after strand of his thick, hot cum deep inside of me. "Fuck, Ava, if that's hate. I would love to see what love tastes like on you." He gasps in my ear as he falls across my body in a heap.

The words crawl around my numb brain. I wasn't sure I knew what love was or why he wanted to taste it. Wasn't he supposed to hate me for what I did? What happened to him hating the girl who tricked him? I was right all along. Chase was dangerous and if I wasn't careful, I would stumble and fall.

I couldn't fall. Not for him. I had protected myself for this long. I didn't believe in fairytales. They were just stories in books. I couldn't fall because I knew he would never be there to catch me.

I couldn't fall.

16

CAPTIVE

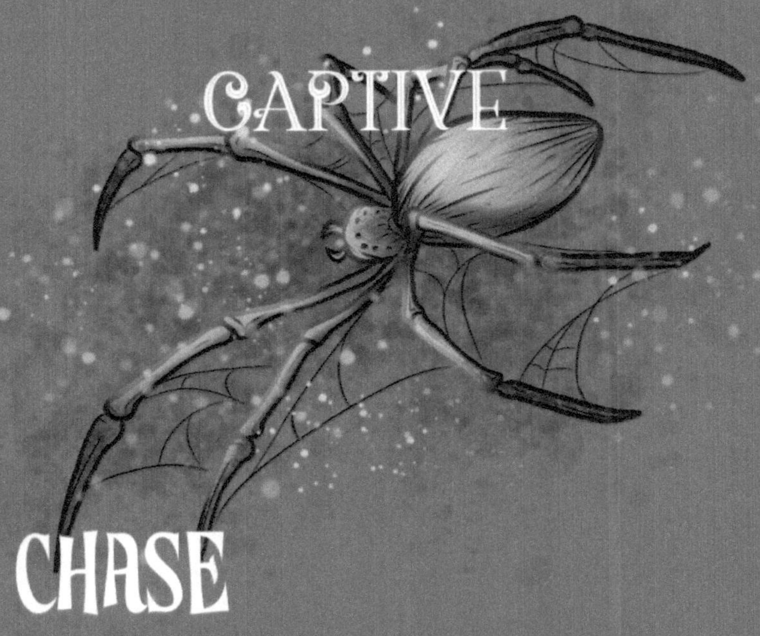

CHASE

I knew there would be animosity, and I was ready for it. Ava had been a sore topic at the Knight table for months. Damon wanted me to forget about her and deal with the shitstorm I had created, but I knew I couldn't do that. I couldn't forget her. I could never forget her. I hadn't forgotten her in ten years.

I didn't believe in that fate bullshit. It sounded like hogwash to me, some lie that women would tell themselves, hoping one day they'd find that person. That perfect person who was just right for them. That person would show up and show them why it never worked with anyone else because their heart was waiting for that person to show up, but that was bullshit, right?

I walk through the wine cellar with her in my arms, looking down at her beautiful porcelain face, her long thick hair of sunlight strewn across my body and her chest rising and falling in her deep slumber, and I'm not so sure anymore.

With every step I take, I know I'm running out of time. I suppose I could just hide her down here and hope that Damon never stumbled upon her, but I was still receiving the backlash from the last secret I had kept from my brother. He couldn't understand why I wouldn't accept the truce that was offered to us. Nikoli was desperate for Ava and I was just supposed to hand her over like she was last night's leftovers. No, I wouldn't do that.

She may be a beast, but she was my little beast.

I take the steps because I'm unsure if they are home and will cause a scene as soon as they see the little bundle I carried in my arms. I remember in the forest when I laid her beneath me, sated and satisfied, and worry crossed her face. "You will not let me go, will you?" I had shook my head. "Are you going to hurt me?"

Those very words sent a stinging sensation to my chest. I knew I was a bastard, but how could she ever think that I could hurt her? The words had floored me. "I would never hurt you. I promise." I had hoped to see relief, but once more worry had crossed her face.

"Yeah, I heard that one already." She muttered before her eyes had shut closed from exhaustion and then it was my turn to have worry cross my face. Someone had promised they wouldn't hurt her? And then they had? I had so many questions but I couldn't ask her. The rage pounded through my body once those words had left her lips.

Nobody would hurt her again, not while I was around. I knew this wasn't the life she had envisioned for herself and that I had ruined her little slice of paradise with my selfish obsession. I should have left her. She had looked so happy when I had been watching her from the forest. I should have just been happy I had seen her again and left like the ghost I was supposed to be. As I had watched her, I knew I couldn't do that. It had taken me so long to find her that when the option arose to walk out of her life—I just couldn't do it.

My stubbornness had put her in danger. I was right all along. She needed protecting—from me and if I hadn't walked into her life, she would have been happy and safe, but my selfishness had put her in danger and now she needed protection from something far worse than me.

I couldn't let him find her. I couldn't let Nikoli take her. I wasn't sure why he even wanted her or where he could have met her. Had she tricked him the way she had tricked me? No, she wouldn't even still be breathing if that was the case. The instructions were Ava was to be brought to him unharmed like a priceless artefact. She was important to him, and that made me want to shield her from him even more.

Nikoli Belvedere was notorious around New York City. The mob boss who ran the entire city. Nothing happened in the city without Nikoli having his nose to the ground, which was why it was interesting that every act I had committed had gone unnoticed. Maybe he had met his match, but that day had never come. He stayed out of my affairs and I stayed out of his. Well, that was until I ended Victor Rossi's life. Then I had his attention, even though that was never the plan. I just couldn't stand there and allow him to defile that little girl.

Death was a kindness to him, but that was one less bastard left to roam the earth.

I remember his daughter Audrey had come to me ten years ago with a problem. Audrey feared her father would capture and harm her, believing that if the sadness didn't kill her, her father would. I wouldn't get involved in Nikoli's affairs. That was the one rule Damon and I had agreed on so that we would be free to run our side of the city. I wanted to stick to that rule, but Audrey had begged, she had begged me to help her and all I had to do was tap into a secure connection that nobody could hack. I wasn't very tech-savvy, but Miles was. Damon secured a getaway that night for her to run, and I secured the area so that she could escape undetected. There was only one rule: I could never know her identity. I was fine with that, but I always wondered what happened to that girl who escaped the entrapment they had locked her in.

I hoped her life was better. That she got the freedom that she deserved. That's why I couldn't leave Ava to her life, not now. I didn't want that life for her. feeling that death was the sole means of escape. That was no life, and she deserved so much more.

I was the lesser of the two evils. Ava would forgive me in the end and if she didn't, at least I would know even through her hate for me I had kept her safe and if that meant she hated me, then I would let her.

Capturing Ava was no longer something I was doing for myself. I had to keep her here to keep her safe. At least here she would be safe. still a prisoner, but safe. I wouldn't let anyone hurt her.

I walk up the cellar steps with her in my arms, no longer anxious that my brother might catch me because this wasn't about him. It was about her and if he couldn't understand that, I would let him believe what he wanted to believe about me. It wasn't about anyone other than Ava, that's all I cared about—keeping her safe.

Opening the door, everything is silent and I creep up the stairs, hoping that I didn't run into one of them because how would I explain what I'm about to do? I picked this room because it was the only room in the house where the window was free from shielding the light. I had learned a lot about Ava during the months I had spent with her and she had an aversion to the dark and I wanted her to feel as comfortable as possible here.

Placing her little warm body on the bed, I hear a sigh pass her lips as I watch her snuggle into the covers I place across her body. So pretty, she looks innocent lying there, unaware that I've done what I had planned to do. I had taken her. I had expected to feel something more than what I felt now, victory, and excitement, but I felt none of that. I didn't even feel the warmth spread across my body. I just felt numb because I had ripped her from her happy place and now she was here, unaware of why I had done what I had done.

Sliding my hands across her face, I slip her hair from her eyes. I had watched her many times like this, and each time, it elicited a new feeling. Like I was seeing her for the first time, something new would overcome my body each time I looked at her this way. She looked so small, like a child you wanted to protect, but she wasn't a child, she was—shit; I didn't know what she was, but I knew one thing. Ava was something that I couldn't let go of, danger or no danger. I had to have her.

I walk away from her and plug the night light into the socket on the wall. I stand there as soft light illuminates the dark room, and it is almost like when the moonlight had illuminated her face. The soft glow around her head makes her look like a pretty sleeping angel, and the warmth that had been missing from my body hits me like a ton of bricks.

Something as simple as just watching her sleep makes me nostalgic for a life I will never have. It makes me feel like I've found a home, but that's a lie. She was here by force. I could never have the version of her I created in my head. All I could have was the lie.

AVA

"Why is this door locked?" I hear a scream from outside of the room.

"Because I locked it." I hear Chase respond.

"Why?" Then silence. "Open it, now."

"No." I hear Chase's gruff response.

"You know, brother, you're pissing me off." Chase had a brother? That was news to me, although I guess in between robbing him and running from him, there was never any conversation about family history.

"Only starting." I hear his smart response.

I hear a twist in the lock and scuffling from outside the door. God, they were acting like children and I was just stuck in here listening to the drama unfold until they both crashed through the door and landed in a heap on the floor.

"Who are you?" The angry face asks me.

"I'm Ava—."

"Of course you are." He smirks. "Nice to see the thief in the flesh." I scowl at his rude comment.

"No offence, but you don't know what you're fucking talking about." I spit back.

"So, you didn't steal from my brother?"

"Well, yes but—,"

"Like I said, nice to meet you, thief." I shake my head because what was the use of trying to defend myself? He was as stubborn as Chase. I watch as they both scramble to their feet. "You," He turns to Chase. "Explain." Chase shuffles his feet nervously. "Chase Knight, you better have a good fucking excuse for bringing her here." He screams at him.

"You know why she's here." He grits back at him.

"Great. Would one of you like to explain to me why I'm here?" I interrupt.

"You didn't tell her?" The angry brother scowls at Chase. "Why didn't you tell her?" He waits, but Chase doesn't respond. "Wait, how did you get her here if she knows nothing?"

"Look, Damon," I watch as he pushes his fingers through his hair. "I don't think now is the time to discuss this." He grits out while giving his brother a stern look.

"Of course you don't." He knits his brows together. "Are you hungry?" I just stare at him and I don't even notice that he's walked towards me until he's clicking his fingers in my face. "Hello, thief girl. Are you hungry?" He asks once more. I nod, "Come on, then." He sighs.

"Wait, you're letting me leave the room?" I ask.

"Try escape," He whispers. "You won't get far."

"Charming," I mutter as I swing my legs from the bed and stand there looking at Chase. "I just—." I look down, not daring to look into his eyes. "Wanted to say thank you for—." Shit, why was this so hard? "The light." I gasp out.

I wait for a response, but one never comes. As I direct my gaze towards his eyes, I notice him clearing his throat. His mouth opens, but then it closes again. Well, this was awkward and the most quiet it had been between us. What had changed? And why did I care? I was his prisoner, not his girlfriend. I meant nothing to him and yet what he had done by placing that light by the bed meant the world to me.

I walk out of the door and breathe a sigh of relief. He walks in front of me, guiding the way. He still hasn't spoken a word. In the forest, I couldn't get him to shut up and now here he takes a solemn vow of silence. It was oddly unnerving. I take in my surroundings as we descend the cream and gold staircase, chandeliers with pretty crystal lights hanging from the ceilings. There isn't much of a colour scheme going on here. Everything is just cream and gold, like they have dipped it in luxury. I can sense the plush cream carpet bounce beneath my feet and it brings a feeling of comfort.

Venturing into a vast hallway, my eyes roam around the area and eventually focus on a door located at the far end of the hallway. A door to freedom. My eyes linger on the door for a little too long and he's noticed. I experience his arms wrapping around my waist and his warm breath causes a delightful sensation up my spine. "Oh, little beast, I dare you." He challenges me. "There is nothing for miles and I sure would love to hunt you again." He whispers. I shake my head and let my eyes move from freedom and back to the place I was stuck in. "Come on, they don't bite." He smirks.

I wasn't sure who 'they' were, but I should hope they didn't bite. We're there, a pack of animals awaiting me in there. I think I should have just taken my chances alone, baked, in the forest because here in this strange place I was out of my element and I didn't like it.

I move behind Chase as we enter the dining room. This room seems more welcoming, with burgundy and cream walls and exquisite curtains draping from the large bay window that streams in a wealth of light that seems to illuminate the true beauty of the room. A large mahogany table sits in the middle of the room that could fit many guests around it and an exquisite chandelier drapes low, allowing the golden light to encompass the room in a dazzling glow of illumination. Positioned at the head of the table, I observe the irate brother from earlier. A beastly man sits next to him and a smaller version of the beast appears even more out of place than I do, but it wasn't the men that surprised me.

My eyes widen as I cast my gaze upon the delicacy on the table. There are pancakes dripping with syrup. Eggs, sausages, bacon. Toast. There are hot cups of coffee just simmering away. Plates upon plates of food that made my tummy rumble and my mouth salivate. I had never seen such an array of delicious flavours all at once. "Wow," the words tumble out of my mouth before I can stop them.

"We didn't know what you liked to eat. So we made every-thing." The angry brother announces.

"You made—all of this for me?" I choke out.

"Yes, well, Chase is an idiot. You didn't ask to be here. I'm Damon. Please sit down." I nod and take the seat opposite that has been offered to me. "I'm the fuck ups brother." He smirks. "That big bastard over there is Gage." He nods to the beast, who gives me the brightest smile I've ever seen. Oh, not so scary after all. "And this little shit is Miles. Don't let his innocent looks fool you." He winks.

"Asshole," I catch Chase murmur.

"So you didn't fuck up?" Chase lowers his head. "what I thought." Damon smirks.

"So, are you all brothers?"

"Well, no," Gage responds. "Well, not blood brothers anyway, but we look out for each other, so I guess we are like brothers."

"How did you meet?"

"Eat." Chase growls, scolding me. I sense the heat rise and notice the heat spread across my face. Grab a plate, collecting everything laid out on the table. I then take a forkful of bacon and quickly eat it, shaking my head at my own lack of restraint in speaking out of turn.. I wasn't even a guest. All I was an inconvenient prisoner.

"Good Girl." Chase smiles. God, why do those words create warmth and a desire to spread through my body? "We met Gage when we were on a job. Damon and I work alone, and Gage was doing the same job. Instead of working together, we fought each other, which could have ended for all of us, and if it wasn't for the enemy launching a sneaky attack, then we wouldn't be sitting here today."

"Oh wow, so it was like fate you would meet."

"I don't believe in fate, Ava. We had a common interest, and we worked together."

"So, fate then," I smirk. I listen to a groan pass his lips. "What about Miles? How did you meet Miles?"

"Oh, Miles was also a happy accident." Chase smiles. "We were down a tunnel,"

"A tunnel?"

"Oh, yes, Chase loves his underground tunnels." Gage groans.

"And you don't?"

"Fuck no," My brows furrow. "Rats, can't stand them." He shudders.

"Me neither," I whisper.

"Anyway, tunnels are the fastest way to move around the city without getting seen. I was down there minding my own business when this little fire starter was planting TBIEDs."

"What's that?" I ask.

"Tunnel-borne improvised explosive device." Miles smirks.

"Why were you blowing up a tunnel?"

"Fun," He laughs.

"Anyway, I was livid when I stumbled upon his little artistry because if he blew up this specific tunnel, then I would have no way of getting through the city underground. Found out he was an orphan so I took him home. Everyone loved him." Chase announced like that wasn't the sweetest thing I had ever heard.

"You've been together ever since?"

"Sure have, little lady," Gage utters. "We might not be blood, but we are family."

"Yeah, a dysfunctional family." Miles laughs while flinging eggs across the table in Gage's direction.

"You're all lucky to have found each other. I never had that."

"Had what?" Chase asks me, but I'm not sure if I want to answer. His piercing gaze never left my face, waiting for me to open up the way he just had, but my story was never a happy one and I didn't want the smiles to turn to pity.

"A family." I whisper.

Silence flutters around the air, and nobody speaks. My words just linger in the air, killing the mood. The once radiant smiles turned to solemn, sad faces, and the pity I wanted to avoid was clear in all of their faces. I wished I could take back the words that had fallen from my lips, but that's the thing about words. Once they were out, there was no taking them back.

"Well, you could always join our family." Miles offers.

"Don't be stupid." Damon spits out. "She's not here by choice, she's here because—well, it doesn't matter why she's here."

"She's here now, so why can't she be a part of our family?"

"She will run the first chance she gets." Chase sneers.

"Maybe she will surprise you."

"That I very much doubt."

Chase was right, given the chance I would run because I didn't belong here. He only brought me here because his revenge plan had fallen through and he still hadn't got what he needed from me. Once he knew there would be no reason to keep me here, he could let me go and find the peace that he had been looking for.

"He's right," I mutter. "I would run. I don't belong here. I'm only here because Chase wants revenge for what I did to him a long time ago, and I never explained why I did what I did." I place my fork on my plate and look at him. "I thought you would have forgotten about me. I thought you would have moved past what I did, but you didn't." I sigh. "When you have your answers, you will find peace—."

"No, Ava, that's not—."

"So, I'm going to give that to you. I owe you that much. What you did was cruel, Chase, but I guess I can't blame you. What I did to you was so much worse. I stole from you that night. That was the goal all along, but I didn't want to."

"You didn't want to?" Damon shouts across the table. "Then, why did you?"

I wasn't sure how I could explain why I did what I did without divulging information about my painful past. That was nothing to do with Chase, and I didn't want to go over the details anymore. I didn't want to think about how my life was back then; I had survived, and I wanted to be a survivor. I didn't want to be pitied. I wasn't a victim. My stupid decisions had put me in danger and I only had myself to blame for that. I wasn't a victim, and I didn't want to be seen as one.

If I didn't get out the words, I needed to right now; I knew I would never say it to him, and I needed to tell him. Not just for him, but for myself. I had held onto this for long enough and I wasn't expecting forgiveness, but he deserved to know why the girl he had shown kindness to have deceived him.

I glance up at him. I'm unsure if the words are even going to come out. "Ava, you don't need to do this." He reassures me. "That isn't why you are here."

"Isn't it?" He shakes his head. "Well, I think you deserve to know, anyway." He stands and walks towards me, sitting beside me. Confusion passes over my face. Great, as if it wasn't hard enough. Now I had to smell him while I tried to go over why I had thrown the kindness he had shown me in his face. "That night, you were the first person in my life to give me something. Something that held value. I never forgot that."

"Ava, honestly, you don't need to do this." He speaks more forcefully this time.

"I won't tell you why I did what I did. I can't tell you that. I had to steal from you that day," I gasped. "My life depended on it," I whisper. "I want you to know that I never touched a penny of your money and everything I have done in my life. That was my one regret." I look into his eyes and they soften. I didn't deserve his softness, I didn't deserve his forgiveness. A lump forms in my throat and I can feel the sting of the salty tears drip down my face.

"Why didn't you tell me." I shake my head. "Fuck. Ava, why didn't you fucking say something. Anything." He speaks. I feel him cover his large hand across mine and I feel his warmth hit my body, but I don't deserve his warmth. I don't deserve any of it.

Pulling my hand away from his, I see uncertainty in his eyes. Pulling the chair back, I stand. "Now, you know. There is no reason for you to keep me here. You can let me go now, Chase. I'm sorry it took me so long, but I hope you can find peace now." I turn and walk away from him.

"Ava," I hear him scream. Stopping at the door, I don't turn, but I stop. "Ava, come back." I shake my head and walk through the door into the hallway. Standing there, I look at the door and it no longer feels like freedom because where would I go now? It was just a way out to be the girl I had always been.

Lost.

I feel his hand on my back. He doesn't grip me or try to pull me towards his body. There is nothing forceful about the way he touches me. There is only a gentle touch full of kindness. Kindness that I don't deserve. "You have your closure now, Chase. You can let me go." I whisper.

Spinning my body around, he pulls my body against his chest. "I can't do that. I can't let you go." He rasps. His fingers slide through my hair, caressing my head. "It was never about the truth. It was always about you, little beast. I can't let you go." His lips press against my head. "I can't ever let you go." He whispers.

The warmth I had denied myself swirls around my head. His words fall across my body and I realise it wasn't revenge he wanted. I had given him everything I thought he needed, but it seemed the only thing Chase Knight wanted...

Was me?

18

BREAKFAST MANNERS

CHASE

Ava had been staying with us for three months and for three months I hadn't touched her. Seeing her every day was torture, remembering how she tasted, how she felt. Shit. Even how she smelt. Having her in my house was fucking torture, but I promised myself I wouldn't touch her, not now.

As I make my way to the kitchen, the aroma of coffee and eggs fills the air. It smells delicious, not the usual smells that come from the kitchen. The scent wafts across my senses and my feet walk towards the delicious smells coming from the kitchen. As soon as I step into the kitchen, I'm confused. Gage is standing there, but as my eyes trail across the area, I don't see Gage. All I see is fucking legs. A groan squeezes from my throat.

Shit. There she stands, in my shirt. Fuck, she's wearing my fucking shirt, swaying her hips as she makes eggs at the cooker. The white shirt curves just covering her delectable ass, and her gorgeous legs sway with her body. There isn't even any music playing. What was she dancing to? My legs move towards her body, enticing me to get closer even though I know I need to move as far away from her as I can. Especially now, with her dressed like that. In my fucking shirt. Shit. Did she know what she was doing to me right now?

My steps quicken but are quiet. I hear her turn the hob on the cooker off and allow her to spoon her eggs onto the plate. My hands move up her smooth, toned legs and I detect her gasp. "You're wearing my shirt, little beast." I breathe into her neck. My body presses against hers and my hand snakes up her neck, pulling her head against my chest.

"I'm sorry," I hear her utter. "I will take it off." A small smile curls across my lips. My hand moves down the buttons, undoing each one and spinning her body around to face me so that I can see how delicious she looks in the morning with my shirt hanging from her body. Lifting her slight frame in my embrace, her arms encircle my neck as I place her on the kitchen counter. With her legs spread wide and her toes gripping the counter's edge, I hear a gasp escape from her body.

Kneeling before her, I gaze at her glistening pussy, allowing my eyes to wander across every little drip of the juice on her pretty pink pussy. "God, you're fucking beautiful." Her face turns a pretty shade of pink and she looks away from me. "Oh no, pretty girl, you look at me when I make you cum." Her eyes are still facing the opposite wall and I'm just so desperate for those enchanting eyes to look into mine, begging me to touch her. I need to see the desperation in her eyes. My fingers grip her chin, pulling her head down to meet my eyes. "Now, look at me while I fuck you." I growl.

"Chase, I don't think—." My fingers dip into her pussy, and she feels so fucking good clenching around my fingers. "Oh god," she cries out. "I—I don't think we—fuck, why are you so; fucking—oh, please don't stop." She screams. "Please don't stop."

"Come here, baby." I gasp, pushing her body closer. "Look how you open up for me." My hands grip her thighs to keep her legs wide for me. My tongue glides up open pussy lips. Her legs shudder in response. "It's okay baby, you can cum as many times as you need to today." My lips clamp down hard against her pussy while my tongue massages her pussy. The screams fall from her body as my tongue laps up every bit of her pretty little pussy. "So, fucking delicious." I gasped, bringing my head up, "But this isn't working." Confusion passed over her face. "This—just—isn't; working; for—me." I pant. While gripping her around the waist and walking with her in my arms to the dining room.

Positioning her on the table with a smirk on my face. "Chase, what are you doing now?" I ignore her and lay her flat while spreading her legs. "What if someone comes in?" Her lips tremble as she looks up at me with worry.

"Don't worry, baby, I don't fucking share." Grabbing the black rope, I tie her legs down and marvel at how pretty she looks spread wide for me. "You are fucking mine and nobody else will touch you—." I bind her arms above her head. "Ever again?" I whisper in her ear. Lighting candies and displaying them round her body so she's basked in a pretty glow of light.

As I strip my clothes, I notice her eyes widen. Witnessing her in this state filled me with excitement, but the intensity in her gaze unleashed my primal instincts. Creeping beneath her legs, her eyes stay fixed on me as I climb up her form. The sensation of her skin grazing mine triggers a surge of excitement on my skin. My thumb slides across her plump pink lips. "Open wide baby," her mouth opens. "Good girl," Her tongue slides out, licking the cock that I've offered her and fuck me. She feels so good. Shivers climb up and down my spine. "Do you want it, baby?" She nods, sliding her lips across my tip and sucking me into her delectable hot mouth. I experience the scorching sensation of her tongue as she glides along with me and vocalizes her pleasure. "Do you think you deserve it?" I gasp. She nods again, my finger thumbs across her cheek as I slide myself out of her mouth. "That's a shame, baby, I don't." I whisper in her hair.

Grasping my cock above her face, her mouth opened in desperation. "I gave you a taste, baby. You don't deserve more than that." She frowns with desperation as I slide my hands up and down my cock, feeling my cock jerk with every intense look that passes across her face. "Oh baby, how desperately do you want to feel my cock sliding down your throat right now." She doesn't speak. The only noise that reaches my ears from her mouth is the desperate little whimpers that escape.

Faster and faster I run my hands across my cock, seeing the desperation in her eyes brings me closer to the edge. "Oh god, baby, it feels so fucking good." I moan, pushing myself closer and closer to her face. Her tongue slides and a smile curls on my lips. "Oh no, baby, you do not get to taste me until I allow you to."

"Fuck, Chase, please." She begs. Her eyes widened with every gasp and moan that fell from my lips. "Please let me taste you." She cries out with desperation and I almost fold, her little cries of desperation almost have me shoving my cock down her pretty little throat.

"Fuck. Almost—there, fuck, Ava." I cry out as I feel my cock pulse and jerk in my palm. The sharp release of desire shoots out of my body, thick strand after strand of cum slides across her face and instead of the look of disgust I expect to see displayed across her face, moans fall from her lips once my cum hits her skin. Seeing the glistening drops of my desire cover her face as it slides down onto her lips. Her tongue slides out, and she tastes my desire across her lips. "I guess you got to taste me anyway, baby." I smile. Running my hands across her face, I smear my cum all over her. She looks so pretty dripping in my cum.

Retracing my path down her body, my hands traveled across her smooth, supple skin. "This might sting a little, baby." I smile. As I lean across and grab a candle, the hot wax pools around the flame, anticipating the beautiful screams that will escape her lips. I tease the candle across her skin, seeing the fear spark in her pretty blue eyes. She shakes her head, and I detect her body tremble beneath mine. "Don't worry, Ava, I would do nothing to hurt—well, not intentionally." I give her a wicked grin.

She shakes her head. "No, Chase, please don't." She begs. With the candle above her breasts, I smile as I tilt it, observing the small drops of wax falling onto her skin. "Fuck." She cries out. "Chase, shit, no." She begs. Once more, I watch as the red wax falls onto her skin, creating swirls of redness. "Oh my god," she gasps. Her eyes widen and I'm surprised at the next words that fall from her lips, "more, fuck, more." She moans. I watch the drips of hot wax hit her skin. Each time the wax splashes against her skin, the moans rip from her throat. Sliding further down until the candle is tipping above her glistening wet pussy. My tongue slides out across my lips. God, she looked fucking perfect. The way her body moves with the dripping wax is beautiful.

Tipping the wax across her pussy, her body thrashed hard against the ropes that bound her to the table and loud piercing cries erupt from her body. "More?" I ask. She doesn't respond. The only thing I can hear is the erotic moans that fill the air. Gliding the wax across her bare exposed pussy once more, observing the drips fall one by one, the screams crash through her body, causing my body to tremble with desire. "Fuck this." I grit out. Untying her arms and legs, I raise her body and hurl her around until I can observe her enticing succulent buttocks mere inches away from my face.

My hand crawls up her neck, and I lean into her body. "You only scream when I want to hear you." My hand presses hard against her mouth and thrust my cock hard inside her dripping pussy. I can feel her hot breath against my palm. When she mumbles her desire, her lips tickle my skin. "Fuck, you are such a good little slut." I cry out. Moving harder and faster inside of her, my other hand grips her hair, pulling her body further into mine and pushing my cock to penetrate her deeper and faster.

"Go on then, baby, scream for me." I move my hand away from her mouth. Gripping her hair tightly in my fist. Her tight pussy clenches around my dick, pushing the desire to rush through me. Her screams illicit the beast inside of me. "Fuck. Ava, cum all over my fucking cock." I cry at pushing deeper and faster inside of her dripping cunt.

"Oh god, oh god—so—fucking; good." She cries out and I feel her drench my fucking cock with her delicious desire. Pushing deeper and faster, I'm so fucking close. The tremors shoot through my body and I hold on to her, dipping my head close to hers until my lips touch her. "Fuck. I'm going to fuck my baby into you. You would look—so fucking good—all swollen from my seed." I feel my desire push out hard and fast deep inside of her. "That's it baby, fucking take it all. Take all my fucking cum. Fuck." I gasp.

I collapse to the side of her, pulling her body close to mine. I just needed her close. I longed for the touch of her fiery skin against mine. It was the only time I felt alive when I had her close to me. I Moved her wet hair from her face and pulled it across her shoulder so I could feel her bare skin, tracing the curve of her spine and curves with my fingertips I heard a contented sigh pass her lips.

I'm not sure how long I lay there with Ava in my arms, but at some point, she twisted around to face me and I got to look into her bright glistening blue eyes that looked at me with wonder. This moment right now was perfect. Basking in the afterglow of sex just looking into her eyes, this was the moment I looked forward to. It was intimate and time would freeze. I never thought she would look at me this way again. Heat travelled to the crevice in my chest and the warmth wrapped around me in a sweet embrace.

"I love you." The words fall out of my mouth before I can stop them. I'm not even sure I want to stop them. Her face twists and I know she's probably confused after everything. "I think through everything, I had already fallen for you. I love you," I repeat once more while stroking her pretty face.

She looks at me with eyes full of tears. "Please don't say that."

"Say what? I love you, I love you, Ava Valentina. I've always loved you. People love to be told they are loved." She shakes her head and I see the first tears fall. "Would you prefer I lied to you?"

"No," she chokes out. "I would prefer you didn't say it all."

"I don't need you to say it back if that's what you're worried about." She shakes her head. "What are you so afraid of?"

"I'm afraid of falling for you. I'm afraid of needing you, but most of all, I'm afraid of losing you and ending up with a broken heart."

"I would never—."

"Please don't say you would never break my heart. On purpose, I believe you wouldn't, but in the end, that's what would happen." She twists out of my grip and climbs from the table.

"Ava," I call out to her.

"It's okay, Chase, just—let's pretend you didn't say what you said."

Jumping from the table, I rush towards her, grabbing her by

the hips and twisting her around to face me. "I don't want to fucking pretend I never said it. I should have said it ten years ago. I don't want to pretend that you make me feel alive and that any second I'm away from you is torture." Grabbing her face, I pull her towards me. "I don't want to pretend because I fucking love you," I growl while slamming my lips against hers.

I feel her body relax and soften against mine. She doesn't resist. This time, she doesn't resist. I press my lips harder against hers like I need to steal the breath from her body. Like I needed her breath to bring me back to life, but after a while I wasn't sure whose breath I had taken, hers or my own. All I knew was she made me feel alive, that every moment with Ava was the only thing in my life that made sense.

"My little light."

<h1 style="text-align:center">19</h1>

WHO IS AVA?

CHASE

I hadn't left Ava since I had brought her home and I wouldn't. I needed to know that she was safe and the only way to ensure that was to see her in my vision. I wouldn't have left her today, but Audrey had left me a frantic call, desperate for help.

I walk to the coffee shop, and the little bell rings on the door as I open it. Scanning the area, I see her sitting there twirling her manicured nail around the rim of the tall white mug, steam wafting across her face as she sits there deep in thought.

"Audrey," I greet her.

"Hey Chase, thanks for coming on such short notice." The way her lip trembles makes me nervous. Nothing shakes Audrey. Nothing.

I take a seat next to her and sit in silence while I wait for her to speak. I knew whatever she was struggling with was hard for her to speak about. She had been more neurotic than normal on her phone call and I knew all I needed to do was wait.

It feels like we sit in dead silence forever and still Audrey hasn't said a word. Every moment I was away from Ava, anxiety pounded my body. I shouldn't have left, but if it wasn't for Audrey, I may never have found her again. I thought I owed her that much, so I had come. I had come.

"Audrey, as much as I love to sit in silence." Her eyes meet mine. "What's going on?"

"Did you find Ava?" I nod. "Is she well hidden?" My brows knit together. "Chase, is she well hidden?" Her tone changes and I hear desperation in her voice.

"Ava is safe, if that's what you mean." She shakes her head. "I promise, Ava is safe."

"Ava isn't safe. She won't be safe again." She speaks.

"I promise, she is safe."

"Do you know why Ava stole from you?" I want to nod, but I still don't know the real reason behind her deception. All I knew was it wasn't by choice and I had never pushed her to tell me anything more. "Chase, do you know why?"

"Ava told me it wasn't what she wanted to do, but no, I don't know the real reason she did what she did. None of that matters now."

"It doesn't matter," Audrey repeats my words and a laugh squeezes from her throat. "It doesn't matter, she repeats once more."

"What's going on?"

"Do you remember ten years ago I asked for your help?" I nod because I had thought about that night and that girl many times. "Do you still not know who that girl was?"

"You wanted to keep her identity secret, and I never questioned your motives," I answer with confusion.

"Yes, I would have kept it that way, but things have changed." Her head bows and she stares into that mug that she still hasn't touched. "That girl who you saved all those years ago." I hear her take a breath. "That girl was Ava." she whispers.

Her words hit me like a ton of bricks. No, that couldn't be true. That girl couldn't be Ava, it just couldn't. She hadn't escaped because I had found her and now—well, that meant. Shit. Why couldn't I just leave her alone?

"No," are the only words I dare utter as I look down at my feet.

"He will find her, Chase. He won't stop until he has her back."

"She doesn't belong to him." I grit out.

"Try telling him that. He found Ava when she was a homeless child on the streets and—." Her voice breaks. "This was a mistake, this was all a mistake. I should have said no to you when you asked me to help you get closer to her. I should have said no."

"Something has happened," I utter. "What do you know Audrey?"

"He's close, Chase. It is just a matter of time before he finds her. Then she will have to relive the nightmare she almost didn't escape when she was younger and this time—." She looks at me with nothing but sadness in her eyes. "I'm not even sure if you could save her." She whispers.

Pain hits my body. All this time, I had viewed her as the enemy, and she was just trying to survive. She wasn't what I had thought she was. Even when I viewed her as my enemy, my feelings had never changed for her. I never wanted to feel anything for the little beast, but she had crawled into my dead-beating heart the moment our eyes had met.

All these years, it wasn't Ava who lied to me. It was I who had lied to myself. So many years wasted on anger, so many years wasted without her because I couldn't admit to myself that she had crawled under my skin that night and while I was busy letting the anger consume me, I ignored the fact that under it all. I didn't hate Ava. Not even a bit, not at all.

"I won't let him have her." I spit back at her.

"I believe that, Chase." She smiles. "I believe you will do everything you can to keep him away from her." She reaches her hand over and taps my hand. "I'm just not sure if your best is going to be good enough—this time."

"You think I can't handle your father?" I smirk.

"I think you've angered the beast and he will raise fucking hell to get back what he believes belongs to him." She pulls her hand away and sighs. "You underestimate how far he will go to get what he wants. He may be my father, Chase, but he is the epitome of evil and I think you—I think you are all in way over your head."

"I won't risk her safety. He won't have her."

"I think you believe that. Maybe not today, but one day he will take her back, and then Ava will be lost to all of us. He won't stop until he gets her. She will always be running and you will be always looking over your shoulder. When you play with the devil, Chase, you get burnt."

Her words sting me. My skin feels like it is crawling. I have never feared anything, but her words bite into my flesh, eating at my soul. I didn't know who he was, but Audrey did and as she sat there, warning me. She was talking like I had already lost, and that chilled me to the very bone.

She gets up from the table and taps me on the shoulder.

"Where are you going?" She stands there, never once giving me eye contact.

"Back home. Ava will be back at some point and as much as she hates me now, when or if she ends up back there. She will need me—again." She sighs. She walks away and never says another word. I hear the bell from the open door and she disappears into the crowd as if she was never here.

The darkness swallows me. I hadn't felt the darkness for many years, but her lasting words plummeted my body into a swirling vortex of darkness. The sadness turns to anger as I sit there. Audrey may not believe that I could protect Ava, but I would die for her, walk through fire before I let anything bad happen to her.

I made a promise that nobody would hurt her and that nobody would ever touch her again and I aimed to keep on that promise I made to her. She was mine. He couldn't fucking have her.

I wouldn't let anyone have her—that little beast was mine.

I groan as I sit in THE BLACK DIAMOND. I never thought I would have to step foot inside of this place ever again. It stained your soul and the longer you spent in its presence, its dark talons would grip your soul, pulling you further into the darkness until there was nothing left but a black hole where your humanity used to be.

"I don't fucking believe it. Chase fucking Knight in the flesh." Cole Lopez is just the man I was looking for. His sandy hair falls across his eyes in curls, his deep grey eyes glisten against his tanned skin. A small smile appears on his lips, no longer clean-shaven, with a goatee shapes his mouth. The clean white shirt is almost bursting through the ripples of muscles that cover his body, tribal tattoos crawl up his bare arms and the signature silver dragon ring curls around his middle finger.

"It's been a while, Cole." I give him a tight-lipped smile.

"How bad is it?" He asks with worry crossing his brow.

"I don't know what you mean," I smirk. "Can't a buddy drop in to see another buddy."

"Not your style, what do you need?" Straight to business, but I wouldn't want it any other way. I was short on time and if Audrey's calculations were correct, I needed to act fast.

"What do you know about Nikoli Belvedere?"

"Shit. Chase?" He shakes his head.

"That bad uh?"

"Nikoli is a crazy bastard. Tell me you didn't piss off that son of a bitch."

"Okay," I smile. "I won't."

"You need information?"

"I need a lot more than that. I need you to secure a safe house. Undetected with no signal to the outside world. Secluded, you know the drill."

"You need to disappear?" I nod. "Shit. Okay, I can do that. Regarding information, how long have you got? Nikoli is bad news. You don't want to get on his bad side. He has his fingers in things we would never touch. I can send over everything I have got." I nod. "How fast do you need the safe house?"

"How fast can you do it?"

"That bad. I got you, man. You know, one day you might drop in and we can have a game of poker instead of life and death shit. One day." He smiles.

"It's a date, Princess," I smirk before I walk away, dreading the great news I would have to tell Damon.

Walking through the doors that had given me so much peace over the last few months. She was like a light. Even Damon had warmed to her and he hated women. It wasn't always that way. A broken heart will do that to you.

I knew it as soon as I had seen Scarlett Anderson. Long dark hair, tanned skin, and a bright smile that softened the hardest of hearts. She didn't belong in this world, but Damon thought he could split this life. But the only thing he had done was harden her heart.

When she had left, I expected him to follow her, but he had just let her go. Never found out why she had left. One minute she was there and the next it was like she had never existed. I didn't want that to be Ava; I didn't want to feel the sting of her presence disappearing from my life.

Walking into the house, I hear my footsteps pound against the ground as I close the door and walk towards the living area. I hear the laughter ring through the house before I even make it to the room. Her laughter wraps me in her sweet embrace, and I smile before I even enter.

Standing in the doorway, she sits with Damon, Gage, and Miles. With cards in her hands, she throws them down on the table and smiles with glee. "Read them and weep, boys."

"God dammit, she must be cheating." Gage spits out.

"Cheating?" She places her hands across her chest. "Why, Gage, I'm offended."

"Sure you are." He mocks.

"Now, don't be sore. Maybe you'll win the next one." She winks.

I couldn't help smiling. She said she didn't fit in here, that she didn't fit in anywhere, but that wasn't true. She fit like she had always been here. She was looking for a family that she didn't think she deserved, but once I brought her here, they had adopted her whether she felt like she belonged or not.

"Oh, Chase, she's rinsing us dry." Miles whines.

"Your playing for money?"

"No, but if we were, we would be broke." Damon laughs. Shit. Is my brother laughing? No, that couldn't be true. Damon didn't laugh, he just scowled and complained about how I fucked up. It seemed Ava had found his humanity. She was good at pulling out the human in you, and I couldn't decide whether that was a good thing or a bad thing. "Where have you been?" Damon asks and just like that, I was about to spoil his good mood.

I walk away from the cheery room and allow the darkness to seep into my soul once more. I didn't need to check to see if my brother was following me because I could hear his footsteps echo behind me.

Walking into the library, I stand by the roaring fire and hear the double doors close. I'm not sure how we all ended up in such a shitstorm. I knew it was my undoing and if I could take the fall for all of them, I would, but this was past them hunting me, now they were hunting something that meant everything I me and I knew they wouldn't stop.

So, she had to disappear. We all had to disappear.

"What's going on?" I hear his serious tone and it's a far cry from the way he was moments ago.

"I met with Cole Lopez."

"Shit. Chase, how bad is it?"

"It's bad, Damon. It's really bad." I turn and watch as he sinks into the armchair, awaiting the horrors that will spill from my lips.

"Nikoli is closing in. He won't stop until he has Ava." His face drops, but he hasn't even heard the worst of it. "Do you remember the girl Audrey needed us to help get out of the city?" He nods. "That girl was—."

He shakes his head. "No Chase," He gasps.

"Yes, and the sick bastard wants her back." Damon doesn't argue with me for once. The realisation is all over his face. We had all risked everything that night for a girl we knew nothing about and not one of us ever regretted our actions. "We leave next week. Cole has secured a safe house. I know it's not ideal—."

"If it keeps Ava safe, we will do it. That's all that matters that she's safe." I must display the shock across my face. "What if I could trade her for you? I would." He laughs.

"Ass," I mutter, shaking my head.

Now, all we had to do was keep Ava safe for a week. That shouldn't be too hard. The danger was closing in and every second we were out in the open was a second he could find her. In a split second, your life could change. One second is all it took for everything I held dear to be ripped away.

One second was sometimes forever.

20

SOMETHING LIKE HOME

I had never uttered the words he wanted me to. He had poured his heart out to me that day and what had I done? I had said nothing. Maybe I was scared if I uttered those words out loud, they would become true.

Once I said it, I couldn't take it back and by saying those words, I was giving him the power to destroy me. I wanted to see the lie hidden within his eyes when he chanted it, but I didn't see a lie. It would have been easier if he had lied, or if he had said nothing at all. I could live in blissful ignorance that we were nothing. That he felt nothing. He had to ruin it by telling me he felt something, and now I was stuck between what my heart wanted and what it needed.

I felt guilty that I had left him hanging, that even though he poured his heart out to me, I couldn't say it back. He never complained or asked why, he just accepted that I wasn't ready to say it. He never once let the idea that maybe I didn't feel it. He just assumed I wasn't ready, like I would be one day. Is anyone ever ready to be destroyed by the person who said they loved you?

I walk through the house, but it is silent. Living with four men, I wasn't used to the silence. I walked to the living area and saw Chase sitting there like he had been waiting for me to enter. "Where is everyone?" I ask.

"Damon, Miles and Gage have gone to prepare for our trip." He sighs.

"Are you going somewhere?" I ask, trying to hide the disappointment that pierces my body.

"We are going somewhere." He raises a brow while taking my hand in his and pulling me onto the settee beside him. "You don't think I would leave you behind, do you?" I shrug my shoulders. "Oh baby, no, I wouldn't leave you." He whispers into my hair.

"Isn't this your home, though?" I ask, with confusion.

"Home is the people you spend it with, not the house in which you live. I will have all my favourite people by my side. So, I will be home. The location doesn't matter, Ava, the people you are with do."

"I never thought of it like that," I mutter.

"One day, I hope you'll come to think of me as home, too."

"I—." I feel his hands wrap around my face and pull my head close to his, his lips covering mine, taking me under. The swirling desire pours across my lips.

"Oh, please stop." I look up and see Miles standing there with Gage and Damon. "It's like watching your mother and father getting it on." He makes a sick face. Holding a cushion in my arms, I launch it towards him. He swings out of the way and Damon catches it in his hands. "Missed me." Miles responds.

"All sorted?" Chase asks and Damon nods. "Perfect, movie night?"

"Why not?" Damon smirks.

Miles skips towards us. "What do you think you are doing?" Chase demands. Miles points towards the spare seat. "Oh no, I claimed this one." He smirks.

"He could have fit on," I whisper to Chase.

"He could, but he's not." Lying on the settee, he pulls my body next to his and wraps our bodies in a cover until it encompassed us in the shawl's warmth that wraps around our bodies. "There," He smiles, "cosy."

They turned the lights down low and everyone settles in their seat and the opening credits of the movie start. Looking at the screen, I watch as the movie starts. A shiver slides up my body as I feel his fingertips hit my thighs. "What are you doing?" I grit out. His fingers dig into my inner thighs and I let out a yelp.

"Are you okay?" Damon asks with concern.

"Oh, yeah, I'm fine. Sorry, I think the movie scared me." I can feel the heat in my face.

"Women." He rolls his eyes and turns his attention back to the screen.

"Scared." I hear Chase chuckle in my ear. "Oh, baby, you are a terrible liar." I feel his grip on my thigh tightens. "Now, be a good girl and spread your legs for me." He whispers. I shake my head. "Don't make me spread them for you." He threatens.

"Please, don't make me do it." I mutter.

"Oh, I'm not making you do anything. If you don't, I will." He whispers. "Either way, those gorgeous legs of yours are getting spread—right now."

I move my legs open, spreading them wider so my legs are resting on top of his. I look around the room, unsure if anyone has noticed what I've just done, but they still glue their eyes to the screen, unaware of what's happening under this blanket. I feel his fingers glide up my inner thighs. "Be silent, baby." He whispers in my ear. My eyes widen as I feel his fingers dance further up my thighs. Slapping my hand over his to stop him from going any further, I hear his low growl in my ear. "Move your fucking hand or I will make you scream and I don't fucking care who hears." I move my hand away from his. "Good Girl," he whispers, causing desire to pulse through my body. "Close your eyes. They will think you've fallen asleep," I do as he asks and let my eyes flutter closed.

That was a mistake, a huge fucking mistake. Once my eyes are shut, it is like every slight touch he causes across my body is heightened and every slight movement causes my body to shake with desire. The way his fingers dance across my thighs has my breath quickening and my heart racing. "Don't worry, baby, I won't make you cum—yet." He whispers in my ear. His words don't comfort me, they have the opposite effect. I could feel the wetness between my legs, and he hadn't even started his tease yet. I wasn't sure if I could stay quiet through his torture-fest.

The excitement slivers up my spine faster than his hands glide up my thighs. Knowing that the others were in the room, unaware, was both horrifying and exciting. I wasn't sure which feeling outweighed the other until I feel his fingers glide up my pussy—shit, I pant. The way he slides his fingertips across my pussy has me biting my lip from trying to cry out. "I—I can't," I whisper. "Chase, I can't stay quiet," I beg.

He dips his fingers into my pussy and still teases me. He barely entered me and my whole body was ready to burst wide open and shoot sparks of electricity through my core. How was this driving me more insane than if he was deep inside of me? I want to open my eyes but I daren't for fear that the moans would fly out of my mouth, alerting everyone in the room to what was happening beneath these covers.

I'm not sure how long his fingers have been teasing me, but it must have been a long time because by the time I open my eyes, I'm soaking wet and we are laid there alone. They have turned the television off and we lay in a blanket of darkness. The strange thing is that even though I'm aware I'm in the dark, I'm no longer afraid. Panic doesn't hit my body like it would. My breathing isn't fast and my heart isn't racing like it's about to win a race. All I feel is a sense of calm surrounding me and I'm pretty sure it's because of the man I'm pressed up against who sleeps with his muscular arms enveloping my body.

This feeling is alien to me, living with anxiety for so long I had forgotten what peace felt like. Where was the impending danger that my body assumed it was in, even when it wasn't? Where was the mass of thoughts that would crawl around my head, making my anxiety move higher up my body until I felt like I was underwater, trying to catch my breath? It was nowhere to be seen. Had I felt the anxiousness for that long that I missed it? Surely not. Calm just sweeps across my body and instead of feeling fearful of an invisible evil, I feel something I have never felt. I feel safe.

I had never felt safe, and the feeling was unusual. I'm sure I was broken. You shouldn't feel like it was a trick to feel safe. Your body's natural urge shouldn't be to run because the man who had been hunting you had given you a safe space. Created a haven within your world that you wanted to run from.

I stir at the side of him and he pulls me tighter against his body. Even in his sleep-induced state, he pulls me closer and I snuggle into his body, allowing him to envelop me in his warm embrace. His lips hit the top of my head. "Sleep," he mutters in his sleepy voice, and I can't help the smile that forms on my lips.

When Chase had spoken about what home meant to him, I had thought he was talking nonsense. How could a person feel at home? But lying in his arms, covered in his embrace, I understood how a person could feel like home because that's what Chase felt like right now, and that thought alone terrified me.

I allow my eyes to close with the thought of how a person could feel at home. This couldn't last. We would part ways at some point. Girls like me didn't get this kind of comfort or safety, but for now, this was something like home.

He was something like home.

He was something like home.

21

GRATITUDE

AVA

One more day to go. We were leaving in one day; I didn't know where we were going or why we were going. All I knew was we were all taking a trip. Chase hadn't said how long we would be gone for. The only thing he had said was, 'We were going on an adventure.'

Breakfast was like every other day, chatter and laughter around the table, which always ended in a food fight. Eggs would fly across the table and you had to duck to avoid the childish banter that would ensue. It was a great way to start the day full of laughter and joy.

Chase had left after breakfast, but I never felt sad when he would leave. I had Gage, Damon and Miles to keep me entertained, here I was never alone. Although I suspected they were instructed to watch me at all times, lest I try to escape. Honestly, it hadn't even crossed my mind. I think if I had left I would miss them, miss him.

Skipping down the steps with a smile, I bump into Damon. He looks up at me and gives me a gentle smile back. "Where are you rushing off to in a hurry?" He asks.

"Oh, you've all been so kind to me." He shakes his head to pass off any heartfelt words that may pass my lips. "I thought I would make dinner for everyone."

"You can cook?" He squints his eyes at me.

"Everyone can cook, Damon. Don't worry, I will not poison you." I wink. "I just want to say thank you for allowing me to stay with you."

"Stay with us?" A loud laugh erupts from his throat. "You came here as a prisoner because my psycho brother wouldn't let you go."

"Minor details." I smile. "I still want to express my gratitude."

"You are a strange girl." He shakes his head. "Come on then, Chase went out. Guess we are cooking."

"Hey, I said I was cooking."

"Fine, I will watch." Yeah, still didn't trust that I wouldn't try to run away. I was right, he was coming with me not for company, but so I didn't escape.

We walk to the kitchen in silence and it is oddly unnerving having someone watch me. I know, strange considering Chase had been stalking me, which after a while had comforted me. I shake my head. Imagine being comforted by a stalker watching your every move. I start by slicing the sides of the chicken breast fillet and stuffing them with cheese, then wrapping them in bacon, holding them together with small cocktail sticks and placing them in a pan, ready to cook for later.

Damon watches my every move, but I'm not sure if it's from interest in how I prep the meal or if he still doesn't trust that I won't run away. It's odd because silence would unnerve me but having him sitting there just watching, it was peaceful.

"You know, you're not what I expected." He breaks the silence.

"No?" I cock a brow. "What is it you expected?"

"I'm not sure." He rubs his chin as if he's deep in thought. "I guess we all just thought you were a thief."

"Well, that's what I was. Just a thief. Nothing more."

"That's not how my brother sees you."

"I'm not sure what your brother sees. He has a strange outlook on everything."

"Don't we all." He smiles while lifting the cup to his lips to take a sip of coffee. Looking at his hand, I see the faded line of where a ring should be. "Your married?" I ask.

He lets out a discontented groan. "Once upon a time, maybe."

"Oh," I go back to pouring heavy cream and cheese into the pan for the sauce that will drip across the chicken. "Well, everything happens for a reason, or that's the lie we tell ourselves."

"Yeah," He smirks. "What was the reason for you stumbling

across my brother that night?"

I think back to that night and I knew it was no accident I had bumped into him. I knew where he would sit; I knew what he would look like. The only thing they did not give me was his name, and he hadn't given that either. Meeting Chase was never an accident. It was all pre-planned by Nikoli. A means to an end, a pawn in his sick game and I was the one carrying out the hit—on his bank account, of course.

No, meeting Chase wasn't an accident. I had thought back to the night many times over the years. It could have been anyone that night, but it was him. Did I believe that fate had thrown us together so that I got one last shot at redeeming my earlier mistakes? Well, I liked to think so.

"Your brother saved me that night," I mumble. "Which makes what I did to him even worse." I stir the sauce and add herbs for flavour. "I never forgot what he did, though. I never thought I would see him again." I let out a sigh. "It seems fate had other ideas."

"I don't believe in fate. We make our own destiny."

"I like that." I smile.

"Yeah," He smirks. "I guess your way of thinking is cool, too. At least if it goes wrong, you can just blame the planets or the moon or whatever it is those hippy girls do these days."

"Hippy girls." I let out a laugh. "It's not strange to believe in something you can't see, Damon."

"Maybe, but if you can't see it, how could you know it exists."

"Faith," I smirk.

"Sure, blind faith." He chuckles. "If he gave you the option to stay or go, would you stay?"

It was a question I had often asked myself over the last few months. Would I stay or would I go? I never had an answer to that question. I didn't know what I would do, because Chase would never let me go.

"Isn't that a pointless question? You know he would never—."

"But if he did, would you stay?" He asks more softly.

That was the question I had asked myself over the last few days, would I stay or would I go? I didn't know. If he had asked me this when I first arrived, I knew without a doubt I would take my chances in the wilderness, but now? I wasn't sure.

Time with Chase was not what I had expected it to be. I had expected to be his prisoner, back to the place I had avoided, shrouded in sadness and trapped in the unsafe net that he had bound me to, but that isn't what he had given me. He had given me safety, and little by little, softened my heart.

"I guess we will never know." I smile.

"Oh, yeah?"

"Chase would never let me go."

Then a smile slips across his lips. "Ava, maybe he would, but maybe you don't want him to." He whispers.

His words slid across my body. Maybe he was right. Maybe just for once—I wanted someone to need me so much that they couldn't let me go. That everything we had been through meant something to him.

Yes, maybe he would let me go.

I hoped he wouldn't, though, and just like that, I had my answer.

If he gave me the option to stay or go...

I would stay.

22

DANCE WITH ME TONIGHT

CHASE

I watch from the door as her fingers glide over the silk-white ribbon that ties the White box together. Her eyes widen and then I see the corners of her mouth upturn into a bright smile reaches up to her dazzling blue eyes. "What's this for?" She asks, noticing my presence.

I walk towards her, wrapping my arms around her waist and placing a slight kiss on her neck. "This, oh, this is just something I picked up." She turns in my arms, looking at me. "It's a gift, Ava. Open it."

"You bought me a gift." Her eyes widen. "Why?"

"That's the great thing about gifts. They are not supposed to be questioned. Now open it." She looks down at her feet before drifting her eyes across my body. She nods.

Slipping out of my arms, she turns and unties the bow. Lifting the box, I hear a gasp fall from her lips. "Chase, I can't accept this."

"Why not."

"It's just—I don't deserve this. You should take it back." She turns away from me and walks towards the window.

My hands slide across her hips, pulling her body close to mine and turning her until I can feel her hot breath tickle my chest. My fingers grip her chin until she raises her eyes to meet mine. "You deserve the world, but we will start with the dress. Never say you deserve nothing, Ava. You deserve everything." The tears form in her eyes and I can't bear to see her cry again. "What's wrong, baby?"

"I—I don't understand why you are being so nice to me." She chokes out.

"Don't start that again." I smile. "Put on the dress, pretty girl." I hear her sniffle and I lay a kiss upon her pretty little head. "I will see you downstairs." I turn to walk away from her, my hand freezes as I reach the door. "I appreciate what you did today. Nobody has ever cooked me anything, Ava." She doesn't make a sound and I don't turn to look at her. "You deserve the world," I utter as I walk away from her.

"Chase," I hear her shout, which stops me in my tracks. "Why do you care so much?" She asks me.

I turn my head and look at her. Even now she looks so innocent standing there looking back at me, waiting for a response. "It's good to care, Ava. It's the only way that you know you are still human." Surprise hits her face, but she says nothing more, so I keep walking and hope that she accepts my gift.

When I went out that morning, I wasn't sure what I was getting. I hadn't even planned to buy her anything. I wasn't one for gifts, but Ava made me want to be that guy. The guy who showed appreciation with gifts, not because I wanted to buy her love but because I wanted to see that light in her eyes that she only got when you surprised her.

I'm standing in town. It feels like I'm spinning around in a circle and I keep passing by all the shops just stuck in the middle. Lost and unaware of why I'm even here or where I need to go next, when my phone rings in my pocket, bringing me back to reality.

The call shakes me to my core. I don't know why because it isn't even something to fear. Damon's words still ring in my head: Ava is cooking us all a meal. Ava was cooking a meal for all of us. My eyes widened. I couldn't believe it, and then I knew where I needed to go. I knew what I wanted to get for her.

It feels like I have been waiting for her to come down forever. I stand at the bottom of the stairs, staring at the space where she should be. She still hadn't come down and the longer I waited, the more anxious I became.

"Will you come sit down?" Damon grits out. I shake my head. "She will not appear just because you're standing there."

"Oh, Déjà vu," Miles shouts. My head turns as I look at him. "Oh, not you. This is brand new to you. I was talking about Damon." I share a look with my brother and pray that he doesn't finish that sentence. "Come on, you all remember, Scarlett." Shit, he had to go there.

Damon looks at him like he wants to murder him. "Miles," I shake my head, warning him to just—stop.

"Yeah, you did this. You stood at the bottom of the stairs and watched while Scarlett—." I hear a crack as Damon's fist connects with Mile's face. He stumbles backwards, holding his face. "What the hell, Damon?"

"Don't do it." I grit out, but it's too late. Miles rushes forward, forcing his shoulders into Damon's body, forcing Damon to stumble and crash on the ground with Miles in tow. I watched them roll across the ground like children that are playing, but they weren't playing. Miles had hit a sore spot, and Damon was unforgiving about the subject that he had broached.

Damon overpowers Miles, which is obvious. He is twice his size. Mile's legs kick out and his face burns red when Damon crushes his head in a headlock. I can see drool fall from his lips as he tries to struggle beneath Damon's firm grip. Miles taps on the ground, but Damon still won't loosen the grip he has around his throat. "Damon, enough," I scream.

"It's enough when I say it's fucking enough." Damon spits back at me. "Mind your own—." His eyes widen and I watch him release Miles from his grip. Miles spits and splutters as the air rushes back into his lungs. Gasping for breath, his eyes also wide and his mouth drops open.

I feel Gage slap me on the back. I shrug away from his touch. "Now, are you going—" Once more I feel Gage hit me on the back, this time more forcefully. Swinging around, I stare into his big brown eyes. "What now?" I scream at him. He points towards the stairs and my eyes glide to where they all watch. There she stands in a royal blue cocktail dress that pulls in all her curves. A cute little blush forms on her cheeks and with each step, I see a sliver of her long shapely legs as they move towards me.

This was the moment, the moment I had been waiting for, and I almost missed it because of Damon's drama. Made a change that someone else had drama for a change. Usually it was me. She glides towards me, but it feels like she's walking towards me in slow motion. I had seen no one look so beautiful, seeing her walk towards me. My heart was in my mouth. It felt like I was seeing her again for the very first time.

I hold out my hand as she walks down to the last few steps. She just looks at my hand and a smirk forms on her lips as she presses her dainty little hand in mine. Feeling her palm hit my skin, warmth spreads through my body. Pulling her against my chest, I breathe in her scent. It swarms all of my senses, pulling deeper under her spell.

"You look perfect, Ava," I whisper into her soft hair that she's pulled into a bun with little tendrils of curls that tickle my face with every movement she makes.

She looks up at me, the swirling hues of her blue eyes gazing back at mine. "Thank you." She utters.

It didn't matter what Ava had; she was grateful for anything you gave her. Even with all the success she had accrued, those little gifts I had left her when I was stalking her were the only time I saw her eyes light up. I realised material things meant nothing to her but a gift that was sentimental meant the world to her.

When we sat around the table and devoured the meal, she had spent all day cooking; I looked across the contented faces and a strange feeling overcame my body. This was alien to me, but she fit in here like she had always belonged. That's when I realised having her here completed this dysfunctional family.

Ava was my home.

The music plays in the background but above the chatter and laughter that spills across the table, you can barely hear the sweet serenade to glides across the room. I had never seen my brother feel more at ease than he was right now, deep in conversation with the woman who had turned my world upside down. I see it. A glimmer. A glimmer of the man he once was, it never lasts but somewhere in there, she had softened him, made him the person he was before someone had ripped his heart out and before the world had hardened him. It was only a glimmer, but a little light in the dark was better than no light at all.

I stand, and the once noisy room turns into a silent shroud of confusion. All eyes are on me as I walk towards her. Her eyes rise to meet mine and that perfect little blush spreads across her face.

"Ava, will you dance with me?" I ask as I hold my hand out towards her.

I'm not sure how long I wait, but it feels like a lifetime passes and I'm not sure if she is going to leave me hanging or not. She looks unsure, but then I feel her small hand slide into mine and relief washes across my body. Nothing I had done here was forced. Every moment that we had she had allowed, it was bad enough I had to take her from her life. I refused to force her to do anything she didn't want to do.

"I didn't know you danced." She whispers in my ear as I guide her onto the floor.

Pulling her body close to mine and feeling every curve fit against my body. "I don't," I whisper. "But for you, I'm making an exception.

For her, everything I had done was an exception.

I didn't dance, but for her, I would dance forever if it meant I could have her body resting against mine. She thought it was just a dance, but having her body pressed against mine was like a dance of two souls.

23

A PERFECT GENTLEMAN

AVA

He holds me close as the music serenades us both in glittering magic. His body pressed against mine is something so exquisitely intimate that causes a fire to burn within my soul.

The candlelight in the room illuminates every feature across his face. I hadn't looked at him, not really, but as his body presses against mine I finally see him. His deep gaze as he looks at me like I'm the only person in the world. The way his eyes dance when he catches me looking back. The way his large hand fits perfectly at the curve of my waist as he slowly moves against my body with the music.

Dancing in his arms, I feel a sense of calm that I've not felt before. Something overcomes me and the warmth of his body pressed against mine makes me feel something I haven't felt—I look into his eyes and my body trembles. "What's wrong, baby?" I open my mouth to speak, but no words come out. A lump forms in my throat and I can feel it tighten as my lip trembles. "We can stop. This is supposed to be nice. We can stop, Ava."

I shake my head and try to let the feeling wash across my body. "It is nice. I don't want to stop." He looks at me like he doesn't believe me, but I can't blame him because I don't even believe the words that come out of my mouth. "I don't want to stop," I repeat, trying to reassure him.

My hand snakes up his neck, and I pull him closer, leaning my head on his shoulders. I can feel his heart race against mine. Our hearts rest together as we slowly away with the sweet serenade of the music and I just away the music to take me away and I do something I never thought I would do.

I close my eyes and I exhale.

I knew that getting close to Chase was risky, but for tonight, I would allow myself to get carried away with the notion that this was real. That tonight, just for one night, everything I felt in this moment was real. Tonight I could pretend this grand gesture was real and the moment we were having right now was real.

I'm not sure how long we stay like this, lost in our bubble, just swaying to the music. Feeling our bodies entwined around each other in a seductive dance that seems to entwine around my soul, he twirls me around the room and a giggle falls from my throat. Even something as simple as a dance fills my heart with joy.

Twirling around until sparks fly into my brain, causing the most exhilarating dizzy feeling in my head. He bends and dips me close to the ground and, for a second; I shake with fear that I may fall. "Don't you know yet?" My brows knit together as I try to figure out what I'm supposed to know. "I would never let you fall." A gasp falls from my lips. "And if you ever fell, baby, I would be right there to catch you." I just look back at him. "You don't believe me?" He smirks as he runs his nose against the length of my neck. "You'll never fall, Ava, the only time I would allow you to fall." He trails light kisses along my jaw. "Is when you fall for me." He smiles.

As corny as his speech was, it was the most romantic thing I had ever heard. Although I think I needed to give him an Oscar for the cheesiest pickup lines known to man. "That line was cheesier than your feet." I hear a bubble of laughter erupt from behind us and remember that while it felt like it was just the two of us, we weren't actually here alone.

"Cheesier than my feet," He cock a brow. "Oh, you'll pay for that."

"Oh, please don't tell me you're going to torture me with your feet."

"No," he smirks while laying my body flat on the ground and crawling across me. "Something far worse than cheesy feet." He grins.

"What could be worse than cheesy feet?" I barely get to finish my sentence before I feel his fingers dig into my ribs and within moments my body convulses in fits of giggles as he runs his fingers across my body.

I had never been tickled before in my life. I know it was strange to go through your entire life to never feel the joy of someone forcing laughter from your body because they want to see you smile.

The breath is pulled from my body and tears stream down my face, but the laughter never disperses. "Please—please, I'm sorry." I gasped out with laughter in my voice.

"Who has cheesy feet?" He mocks.

"You do," I smirk.

"I told you before, Ava, your mouth would get you in trouble." His fingers dig back into my skin, forcing the laughter to fall from my body once more.

"Please. I give in." I gasp out as the tears of laughter crawl down my face. He pauses and looks at me as if to assess if there are any other retorts that want to fall from my lips.

I suppose I could continue with my sarcastic remarks, but I'm not sure my stomach would forgive me. An aching pain from all the laughter had travelled to my stomach, causing my body to tense. "I swear, I give in." Smiling, the sweetest smile I can muster.

His hand comes towards me and I'm about to grace myself for another tickle match I knew I was going to lose. I shake my head. "Please, Chase, I can't—." He holds his hand out once more and clasp my hand in his, allowing him to pull me from the ground.

"I think you've had enough excitement for one night." He whispers in my ear while moving my body towards the stairs.

"Where are you taking me?"

He moves away from my body. "Well, a gentleman always makes sure the lady gets home safely."

"Chase—."

"I'm walking you to your door, Ava."

"Like a date?" I gasped with astonishment.

"Exactly like a date." He smiles.

When we reach the door, this has all the awkwardness of a first date. Even though I knew we were playing pretend, it was fun to imagine that it was real. He moves closer, but he's more careful, as if he's unsure what he should do next.

His fingers gently tease my face but he doesn't forcefully push me towards him, he just lightly grazes my skin and looks into my eyes, gently bringing his head closer to his lips slowly brush against mine and even though it was the lightest of kisses, it was the most tender moment I had experienced with anyone and in that three-second kiss; he took my breath away.

"Goodnight, Ava," he whispers against my lips.

"Goodnight, Chase," I whisper back and I watch as he walks away, barely believing that for the first time, he's not coming in.

He really was a gentleman tonight.

Playing pretend made my heart yearn for more, but as I watched his back until he disappeared out of sight, it made me realise that somewhere between playing pretend; I had found my smile and with that thought; I closed the door and played pretend that he would come back.

24

THE LAST NIGHT

CHASE

The intimate moment I had with Ava made me feel warmth and heat. Our last night in the house was perfect. I wanted to give that to her. Something she could remember, something she could remember with hope. I didn't just do it for her; I needed something to hold on to when the darkness came and it would come. It was just a matter of when.

I hadn't intended to go to her tonight. Everything had been so perfect. The meal, the way she felt in my arms as we danced around the room like we were the only people in the house. Everything was perfect. Even when I had dropped her off in her room and the slight brush of her lips against mine when I said goodnight. Perfect. It was the perfect end to a perfect last night.

I lay on my bed with my hands resting behind my head and I could already feel the lack of her presence. I should be holding her in my arms right now, but she is in her room and I am in mine. There was something wrong with this picture. I jumped from my bed and raced out of my room, rushing down the hallway but stopping in my tracks as I saw her racing towards me.

I couldn't believe it. I wasn't sure if the shock was clear on my face, but it was clear on hers. I walk towards her and her eyes never leave mine, but I see a slip of a smirk appear on her lips. I rush forward and take her face in my hands. I can hear her breath quicken. "Going somewhere?" I smile. She shakes her head as my lips brush against hers, tasting the sweetness from her lips.

Swooping her into my arms, I hear the cutest little giggle fall from her lips. As desperate as I was to have her tonight, I didn't want to fuck her with feverish passion. I wanted gentle, sweet caresses and to feel the warmth of her skin as it pressed against mine. If this was our last night here, I wanted to savour it as sweet as the day we had.

"Chase, did you need something?" She asks once I walk us both back into her room. The room I should have never left earlier.

"Yes, Ava." She peers at me through her elongated dark lashes. "I need you."

The way her body shudders in mine has the desire curling through my body. I want to just devour her, but tonight wasn't about me. It was about making it special for her. She may have asked me what I needed, but what did she need? I wasn't the only one racing down that hallway.

"Do you need something?" I ask her as I lay her body against mine, enveloping her in my arms and feeling her hot breath whip against my bare chest.

"Just this." I feel her smile against my chest. "Just you. This is all I need." She utters. Not quite the words I had been waiting to hear, but they came pretty damn close.

"Oh, baby, careful now. You'll make me soft." I smile as I

run my fingertips through her hair and smiling every time a contented sigh would leave her lips.

"I knew you were soft, anyway." I feel her smirk against my skin.

"Soft?" I can feel my brow rise in annoyance. "Do I need to tickle you again?"

"No, please don't." Flipping her over, I see the smirk slip from her lips. "Chase, please don't." She pouts. My fingers glide towards her body. "No, no, please—." I slide my hands up her body and feel her body relax beneath my touch.

"If you don't like something, I won't do it." I watch her eyes glaze over and all I can see is everything she still won't say to me. Her eyes sparkle as they gaze back at mine and I just get lost in the crystalline magic of her blue eyes.

Sliding my hands further up her body, I hear the groans she's been trying to stifle. My fingers find the straps of her dress and graze across her bare shoulders. Her body trembles with every brush against her skin. "Oh, baby, I love how you respond to me." Her face blushes. "Just like that," I smirk. My lips press against her reddened cheek and I can feel the smile pulling at her face once my lips hit her skin.

Sliding the straps down her arms, I see every inch of her perfect little body as the dress slides down. Moving my body across hers so I can free her from the dress that her beautiful body had filled. Reaching her feet, my tongue slithers and presses against the base of her foot, gliding to her pretty toes. A small giggle falls from her lips. Sliding her toes in my mouth, I suck, massaging my tongue across her pretty toes as they fall in and out of my mouth, and a moan falls from her lips.

My tongue slides out, massaging her feet, and as my eyes peer up at her, I see her eyes fall into the back of her head. A small smile glides across my lips at hearing her erotic moans fill the air as my tongue slips between her dainty little toes. My lips press against her feet, pressing sweet kisses all the way up her feet.

My lips run up her legs, teasing gentle little kisses up her legs. She wiggles her legs when my lips hit her skin, and small contented moans fall from her body. Sliding my fingertips across her legs as I run my lips up the length of her legs.

My fingers tease her face, and I hear a sigh slip from her lips. Looking into her eyes, i just gaze at her. Her beautiful face takes my breath away. I can see her dying to avert her gaze. The longer my eyes linger across her pretty porcelain face, the faster the shyness overcomes her face, and that pretty pink blush stains her cheeks. "Why are you looking at me like that?" She stutters out.

"Why wouldn't I want to look at you, baby? You're beautiful."

"Beautiful?" she gasps. "Chase—I—uh;" Her eyes glitter as the swirl looking back at mine and a smile spreads across my face as I look back at how ethereal she looks gazing back at me.

My hands crawl to her face, curling around her face as I dip my face close to hers. "Yes, beautiful." I smile and press my lips against hers. I was only going to give her a tender kiss, but her lips draw me in, pulling me deeper under her spell, as her lips move against mine with a feverish need. I get lost in the moment. lost in her. My tongue slides in the depths of her mouth and when I feel her tongue hit mine, fuck, the tremors of desire shoot up my spine causing my body to ablaze with heat.

Salivating her taste, my lips press against hers in a feverish need until she's gasping in my mouth, causing my body to curl with desire. I play with her golden hair as I kiss her, pressing my lips against hers. I flick my tongue against hers in slow strokes, making my body shudder as her hot tongue meets mine.

I feel her trembling as my fingers glide down her body. The slightest contact with her velvety skin sends a scorching sensation coursing through me. Burying my fingers into her thighs, slow moans fall from her lips, driving me to the edge and yearning to feel my body press harder against hers.

There were no props, no animalistic actions driving me to the brink of insanity, desperate to be inside of her. There was just me and her, entwined in the sweetest of touches. Enjoying each other's bodies, there was something erotic about just feeling her against me, like her body was serenading me and it was the most beautiful song my body had ever experienced.

"Chase," she gasps into my mouth, my head raises, already missing the taste of her lips against mine.

"Yes, baby."

"Are you trying to drive me insane?"

I shake my head and give a small smile, "insanity, sweet Ava," my fingers tease her thighs, moving closer and closer to her dripping pussy. "Can be—." My fingers keep crawling until I feel them sliding against her wet pussy lips and moans crawl from her throat. "Delicious," I breathe against her lips.

My fingers explore her pussy, the gasps and moans fall from her throat causing her body to thrash against mine. "Oh fuck," she cries out. "So—so—good." She gasps. My fingers enter her tight dripping hole and the screams tear from her body in a mass of deep throaty gasps.

Kicking her legs forward to spread my beautiful princess wide, I can see the slick glistening of her desire coat her pussy. My body slams hard against hers, causing her eyes to widen. "Such a pretty princess. I love how ready you are for me." My hands grip her thighs, pushing against her but not entering her just—yet. "You're fucking eyes make me so fucking hard, baby." I rasp.

"Chase—I—I want this." She gasps out.

"I know, baby, I wouldn't do it if you didn't." I smirk.

Positioning my cock at her centre, I'm so fucking desperate to be inside of her once more and feel how snug her pussy feels around my cock. The sliver of excitement travels through my veins, pushing my body close to the edge. My hands snake back up her body as entwine my hands with hers. "I want to see you this time. I want to see all of you." I plead.

Looking into her enchanting crystal blue eyes that are swimming with desire, with her hands clasped in mine, feeling her warmth travel through my body. I glide my cock deep inside of her tight pussy, the gasp falls from my throat as soon as I enter her. This time it was different, this time it was more intimate. I wanted her to feel how I felt about her. I wanted her to see it in my eyes, feel it in her body.

I wanted her to know, she was mine.

Sliding my hips slowly against hers I hear her desperate moans. She tries to shake her hands out of mine and I let slip a small smirk, never taking my eyes away from hers. Once more she desperately tries to release her hands from mine, I can see the desperation laced within her gaze. "Oh no, baby, tonight I want to hold you." Fear crawls across her face within moments. "I want to see you."

The grip on my hands against hers tighten, the tears are evident within her eyes and I know this is making her uncomfortable. This is too close for her, she doesn't want this kind of tenderness, this kind of closeness but she was going to get it—tonight she was going to get it all.

"Please let me go," she pleads. "Why can't you do it like you usually do?"

"You want it rough, baby?" She nods. "That's a shame, baby, tonight you are getting it slow. So fucking slow that you won't know where you end and I begin."

"Please, Chase." She pleads once more.

My hips gently rock against hers and I feel her squeeze my cock causing a sharp gasp to fall from my throat. "Does it not feel good?" I rasp.

"Yes," she pants. "It feels—so—fucking—good."

Slowly sliding in and out of her tight pussy, I can feel her fingers dig into my hands but I still don't let go. "That's right baby, I can feel—all—of—you." I gasp in her ear. "Fuck, you feel so fucking good." Her moans pierce my eardrum but the sound of her erotic moans just causes my cock to pump with excitement while I slowly move deep and slow.

I could fuck her like this all fucking night long. She felt so fucking good, buried deep within her tight pussy, the pleasure rushes through my body at a rapid rate. It feels like my body is fuelled by electricity running through my veins and the only thing that stops me from losing control is looking into her pretty blue eyes.

She's not the only one who is desperate for an intense, feral fuck. I want it so bad, but I need to give her the tenderness tonight, I need her to know that she means so much more, that she was always more than a fuck to me. Tonight, I want her to feel what it's like to be loved.

"Please, please go faster." She pants.

"No, baby, nice—." My lips graze her neck. "And slow."

"Fuck, why are you tormenting me." She cries rather dramatically.

My fingers entwine around hers, tighter as I glide my cock up and down her soaking pussy. She's covered me in her juice but she feels so fucking good that I don't want to stop. The way she grips me makes my cock shudder with undulating pleasure. "Because little beast, I love you and I don't want to fuck you." Her eyes widen, "I want to love you. All of you."

Moving a little faster I can hear her moans turn to sharp screams. "Fuck, Chase, yes—just—like—that." Her voice in my ear causes my body to keep at the light pace, her body shudders beneath mine with her small thrust that has me pulsing around her pussy. "Oh god, oh god, just—fuck." She cries and I feel her smother my cock with her slick pussy juice.

Her body shakes but my thrusting doesn't cease. Thrusting deeper and slower deep inside of her, her cries of pleasure penetrate my ear. Sharp pangs of pleasure hit my spine as the pleasure crashes through my bod. "Fuck, Ava, I fucking love you." I cry out feeling my thick load shoot inside of her but that's not what makes my body shake. The small tears that crawl down her face as I look into her eyes makes me shake with surprise.

Gasping for breath I fall at the side of her body, wrapping my muscular arms around her body and holding her close, I hear the quiet sobs that she tries to mask by burying her face within my chest. "What's wrong baby?"

"Why did you have to do that? Why did you have to say that?" Her muffled sobs hit my body.

"Why did I have to say I love you?" She nods. "Because silly girl, I do."

She raises her head and tears continue to fall down her pretty porcelain face as she looks back at me. "I can't—."

"I know, baby," I smile. "You don't need to."

I hold her in my arms, and I feel something I have never felt before. I feel happy and I don't even want to run from it—that was Ava's job. I wanted to stay here until morning, look into her pretty eyes when I woke up, but I also wanted to give her the choice.

This wasn't about me. I didn't want to force her into feeling something if she didn't. I didn't want her to feel like she had to lie in my arms, so I wait until she's in a deep slumber and I slowly move her body across the bed, listening to her peaceful little murmurs.

Ava had turned my world upside down and made me whole

again. Something I thought was impossible. As I watch her sleep, I'm amazed at how much I feel about the little beast, but maybe I always had.

I had thought all those years ago hate fueled me, but now I look down at her sleeping frame, I realise I couldn't let her go because I had always felt something for her. It was easier to tell myself that I hated her. It was the best way to not get a broken heart, but I never hated her. I think I just wanted to love her and now I needed to protect her.

As I stand there, I regret moving away from her warmth as soon as I leave her bed. She was so beautiful. This was more than I ever expected she would give me, but when those tears fell down her face, something deep inside of me stirred. It broke my heart that she would rather deny what she felt by breaking her own heart.

She didn't know it yet, but she could never break her own heart because I had taken a piece of her with me, stored in a special place in my chest. As long as I held onto her heart, she could never break it, not fully.

No matter how many times she broke her own heart, I would be there to make it whole again.

25

CAPTURING AVA

AVA

I lay still, allowing the darkness to shroud me. The warmth of his arms around my body was no longer there. Silence suspends me, deep in thought. Seeing him gone fills me with loneliness and sadness.

I had hoped he would still be here and that I would be locked in his embrace. Is that how he felt when I had disappeared from his arms all those years ago? Was this my punishment? But I know I'm been silly, he hasn't disappeared. He had just gone to his room.

The thoughts run around my head. The thought of every moment I've had with Chase buzzes around my brain. Why was I so bothered that he had left? Why did I care? I couldn't understand what had changed, but everything had changed. Since I had been here, something had changed. I just didn't what had been changed.

Laid there in the darkness, I finally realised what had changed. The fear pounds in my chest and I just want to run. Run away from the crawling anxiety that creeps up to my chest. My heart is pounding as the crawling fear climbs through my body at an alarming rate.

The events and the words swirl around my brain, and then it hits me like a bolt of lightning. Like a light bulb had pinged inside of my head. The one thing that I had been denying myself, the reason I had lied to myself for so long. The words I dare not speak out loud, not even to myself.

I loved Chase Knight.

The words spin around my head as if they are on a loop and I can feel the warmth spread around my chest as I finally admit that underneath it all; I felt something for him. Maybe

I always had, and I just didn't believe I deserved it.

The words pour out of my mouth in a rush:

I love him

I love him.

I love him.

I can feel a smile pulling at the corners of my lips and my head swims with warmth as I slide my legs from the bed. The pounding in my chest races harder as I slowly walk towards the door and stall, brushing my fingers across the handle.

Go to him I hear a voice in my head.

I could spend my days with him and never utter a word. He never asked me if I felt anything for him, he never asked me for anything, he was just happy with how things were, never pressuring me to give him what I couldn't or wasn't ready for. I could spend forever, never admitting to him or myself his, I felt, and he would still never force out the words he was already aware of.

Then excitement runs through my body. I didn't want to spend forever as his captive; I didn't want to spend forever, never telling him I loved him. I wanted him to know that despite everything; I felt something for him, too. I couldn't let fear stop me from telling him. If I didn't do it now, then I knew I would never do it.

I'm going to tell him.

Pushing my hand on the handle, I thrash open the door with excitement running through my veins. I can feel every vibration of excitement pierce my body and I rush into the hallway, running towards his room. I feel powerful hands grip me from behind. I can feel his tight grip as my body is crushed against his.

"Nikoli will be so happy to see you." I hear his slimy voice in my ear and fear shoots up my spine. I don't speak, the only thing I can do is shake my head.

I can't move. I'm standing crushed against his body and I can feel the tremors of excitement dissipate. and that excitement is quickly replaced by something I hadn't felt for years. Fear. Not just normal fear, but fear that makes you want to crawl back into a hole you thought you'd never have to hide in again.

He had found me.

I feel his hand snake up my body, but not sexually. He snaked his hand up my body in a domineering way. He had found me and I knew this time I would never escape. As his hand moves closer to my head, I can smell something pungent coming from the clean handkerchief he holds in his grasp.

Opening my mouth, I know what I need to do. I need to scream; I need to alert Chase to the danger I am in and help myself, but as my mouth opens, no sound comes out. Of all the times my body is paralysed with fear, it chooses now.

Scream, scream, scream. I will myself to scream, shout, and make any noise, but with my mouth opened nothing comes out, not even a whimper.

"Don't worry. You will be back home before you know it." His slimy voice threatens. While bringing his hand closer to my mouth.

"I never got to say I love him." I finally mutter before I feel his hand pressed hard against mine and the fumes from the cloth he holds in his hands hit my body instantly, making my head spin.

The only words I had to speak were ones spoken with regret. I would never get to tell him how much he meant to me. I would never get to tell him he had saved me. I would never get to tell him anything because now I had to go back to the nightmare I thought I had escaped.

Nikoli had stolen that from me, too. He had stolen my chance to tell Chase that I loved him. I had waited too long and now he would never know. He would think I had run away and now he would never know.

I can feel my eyes slipping and the darkness coming. I knew I didn't have long until the darkness consumed me and the same thought travelled around my head as if I have played it on a loop.

He would never know.

EPILOGUE

NIKOLI

Pacing the room, I finally found her. My little girl was coming home and I couldn't wait to see the look on her face when we came face to face. Still wasn't sure how she had escaped or evaded me for so long, but that no longer mattered.

Ava was coming home.

Chase thought he had outsmarted me, that he could keep my little girl hidden from me forever, but what he hadn't realised was—in the end, I always win. I thought he would have accepted my truce. Shit, even offered the stubborn bastard a reward, and he had still left me in silence. It wasn't easy finding where he had her hidden, but when I found her, I knew revenge on that low life didn't matter. Losing her would be vengeance enough.

I had found her first. He couldn't keep her. She belonged to me and this time I would make sure she never slipped through my fingers. When she came back home, she wouldn't be leaving.

Of course, I knew he would come looking for her. That was something I was rather looking forward to. Then she could watch him die at her feet. That would be her last lesson for defying me and running away. Take away their safety net and they would never feel safe again. The only safety net Ava would ever get to depend on again was mine, but she would have to earn that.

"You found her then?" I hear Audrey interrupt my manic thoughts.

"Did you ever think I wouldn't?" I smirk.

"No, of course not, father. You are brilliant. I knew you

would find her."

"Oh, don't butter me up, child. Don't think I didn't notice your disappearance, too."

"I was sad. She was my only friend." Her eyes are full of sadness and I take a step back. I guess I had never thought about how Ava's disappearance would affect her.

"Of course you were." I put my hand on her shoulder. "Well, we are all back together again. Like a joyful family reunion." She nods and walks away from me.

Audrey had been like a ghost since Ava had left. It was like I had lost both my girls, but Audrey would still come if I asked too, but a niggling feeling still gnawed at me that Audrey didn't want to be here. Now that Ava was coming home, I knew she would never leave and finally, I would have some order back in this house.

I hear the door and excitement travels through my body. Not long now and I would have what belonged to me. I can hear the tapping of shoes on the floor outside the door. As I stand near the roaring fire, I'm enveloped by its warmth. I had never been unsure of anything but meeting Ava again. After all this time I'm unsure his she will react. She was no longer the young girl I had in my arms. She was now a woman—my woman.

The anticipation of her arrival makes me impatient. What was taking so long? I knew she was just beyond that door and she had yet to walk through it. I hoped she would have missed me and that she was filled with regret for ever leaving me. The anger hits my body, but I have to stay calm and in control. What she had done needed to be forgiven and, in time, I'm sure it would be.

The doors handle comes down and the large oak door swings open, but nothing but silence follows. Slowly turning around, I'm met with an empty space and confusion hits my body. Where was she? I had waited all day for this moment and I still had yet to see her.

They ushered her body into the doorway, and it sucked my breath from my body. Ava had always been a mystery to me. But the woman who stood before me was downright mesmerising. My eyes crawl from her bare feet, lingering up her long-toned legs I had often enjoyed sliding across my shoulders. Pimples of desire shoots through my body. Her long golden hair flows down her body in waves, her plump mouth forms into a repulsed grimace, and those dazzling icy-blue eyes penetrate my body with all her hate.

Walking towards her I can sense her body stiffen but even I know she must realise she has nowhere to go, she is back home and she can't leave. I had hoped she would at least look happy to see me. If it wasn't for me, she would have died that night in the blistering storm. Ungrateful.

She doesn't move. She doesn't speak. She just stands there staring back at me like she hates me, maybe she hates me but she would learn to love me—one day she would love me and if she didn't, there was no way I would ever to walk out of here. The only way Ava would ever leave me would be in a box.

As soon as I reach her, I'm swarmed by the scent of honey and sweetness that emits from her pores, enveloping my body in her essence. It is a scent I had longed for over the years and being so close to her with her scent swirling around my body, warmth hits my body.

My fingers glide across her shoulders and a scowl crosses her pretty little face, and she shrugs away from my touch. This action alone both surprises and excites me. Young Ava wouldn't have dared to deny me what I wanted, but this Ava—this Ava was a delightful surprise.

Once more, my fingers hit her shoulder and once more she shrugs away from my touch. The feeling of her silky hair between my fingers for only a mere second sends shivers coursing up my spine. Gripping her by the chin, her head sways, trying to get away from my touch, but this just makes me grip her harder. Hate pools from those baby blues.

"Hello, little girl. Welcome home." I utter.

Forcing her body from the doorway and into the room I feel her shudder beneath my touch and leave her standing in the middle of the room, I turn back towards the door sliding it, and I spot Audrey looking back at me and before I close the door, I give her a smile.

Hungry for more?

Grab my next release.

One Night Stand:

I like my women how I like my life; fast and loose.

Cain Callahan is the oldest of three brothers.
Cain was born into the family business but unlike his broth-
ers, he didn't care much for rules.
His reputation has been tarnished by his erotic lifestyle.
Tarnishing your life is fine but when it seeps into the family

name, that will not do.

Daddy is not happy and Cain has to pay the price.

Cain has lived a luxurious life in New York but his family has grown tiresome of his lack of business attitude and when a meeting is called, it is decided that Cain will set up in London with his brothers.

Aideen is as fiery as the sun.

She's just supposed to be a one-night stand...

So why has this one crawled under his skin?

Aideen is about to teach Cain that not all women are the same...

Will one night really be enough...

The first in Calia Quinn's heart-thumping London Playboy series which can be read as a standalone.
The Callahan brothers will have you falling into those toe-curling moments that will leave a lasting impression

that proves even bad boys deserve a HEA.

Available on amazon.

Calia Quinn is a romance writer from the united kingdom.

Calia's Debut released October 2023

Calia creates stories with sassy heroines and morally grey men, with a mixture of steamy and humorous moments between her characters.

Calia has always had a love for the darkness.

In the dark, there is a beauty which is why the dark element in her tropes is present.

Calia's favourite romance has always been dark romance.

Who doesn't love a morally grey anti-hero?

When Calia is not writing, you will find her reading a mixture of tropes but almost always these involve romance because who doesn't love a happy ending?

You can find the author:

amazon.co.uk/Calia-Quinn/e/B0BZ3YS1XN/ref=aufs_dp_fta_an_dsk

tiktok.com/@caliaquinnauthor

facebook.com/caliaquinn

instagram.com/caliaquinnauthor

g goodreads.com/author/show/29969021.Calia_Quinn

You can visit the author's website:

https://www.caliaquinn.com